THE BLANCHARD BROTHERS
FILM COMPANY

A NOVEL BY

R. D. SNOWCROFT

**HAMPSHIRE HOUSE PUBLISHING CO.
FLORENCE, MASS.**

All rights are reserved. Except for short excerpts for the purposes of a review, no part of this book may be reproduced, stored in a retrieval system, or transmitted in any form or by any means, whether electronic or mechanical, including recording and photocopying, without the written permission of Hampshire House Publishing Co. For permission, contact:

>Hampshire House Publishing Co.
>8 Nonotuck Street
>Florence, Mass.
>01062

First printing

Manufactured in the United States of America

Copyright © 2007 by Hampshire House Publishing Co.

ISBN: 978-0-9636814-7-8

Library of Congress Control Number: 2005931532

THE BLANCHARD BROTHERS' PLAYERS

Estelle Harrison

Bill Trowbridge

Marion Fiske

Margaret Eagan

Frank Eagan

1.

The automobilist

In the spring of 1911, a motordrome was completed on the Newark fairgrounds in New Jersey, and Carl Milford, who had made a name for himself in the Vanderbilt Cup races on Long Island, was hired to take on the challenge of the era's great racers weekly.

A demonstration of Milford's Benz racer on the track was scheduled for invited guests and the press. The course, a quarter-mile, saucer-shaped affair constructed of pine boards, surrounded a pond and magnificent water fountain.

The Blanchard Brothers Film Company, which had just taken up residence in the former Bergen Creamery nearby in Fort Lee, planned to make its first film with the racing exhibition as a backdrop, so a notice requesting actors and actresses was posted in a booking agent's office in Manhattan.

One who saw the listing was Estelle Harrison, an actress of no great name in the theatre but of some experience. She was thirty-five and had been acting for more than half those years, mainly in road companies traveling the Midwest.

Tall and somber-eyed, she was a character actress employed most recently at the Knickerbocker Theatre on Broadway in a production that lasted only eight performances, *The Maid's Maid*. Never a lead on Broadway and rarely even the second leading woman, she had played the fourth maid.

At an age when finding even small stage roles was growing increasingly difficult, Estelle had begun to worry that she would end her life in the poverty in which it began. However, exactly a year from that morning, two women, one a cousin of William Waldorf Astor, would stand outside a movie theatre on 57th Street studying a Blanchard Brothers movie poster prominently featuring an illustration of Estelle. They would debate a phrase running along the top of the broadside: "Aunt Jane, the most beloved character in moving pictures." Was she more beloved than, say, the Thanhouser Kid or Moving Picture Mary at Biograph? That was the question that would engage the two women a year hence with a seriousness worthy of a point of philosophy or religion.

Now, though, as Estelle stood before the nearly

empty booking agent's board, she could not have anticipated such an occurrence, and although it was a humiliation for a theatre actress of any seriousness to appear in motion pictures (and she never had), she could not ignore the listing. She was between jobs, rent had to be paid, and her savings were vanishing. Reluctantly, she wrote down the card's information.

In a heavy fog that did nothing to mask the unpleasant smells of the Hudson River, Estelle took the 125th Street ferry from Manhattan over to New Jersey, then an electric streetcar to the film studio. It was on boarding the trolley that she recognized Margaret Eagan, whom she had met only once before, at a lap supper given by a mutual friend. The young actress approached her and they exchanged pleasantries. They talked about the lean times in the theatre and the lack of roles. Margaret said she was modeling furs on Second Avenue in the evening and going to auditions during the day.

"There's nothing out there. I know actors renting half their bed to strangers," Margaret said. "Some are eating meals of horse meat and shoplifted vegetables. So what's your business today in New Jersey?"

Estelle lied, saying she was going to see friends. Margaret said she was visiting an aunt.

When the trolley reached Linwood Avenue,

where the film company was located, they both got off and began walking alone on opposite sides of the street, waving awkwardly to each other from time to time. After two blocks, it occurred to Estelle that they were both traveling to Blanchard Brothers and were equally ashamed of it.

She called across, "My dear, are you on your way to make movies?"

Margaret stopped. "Oh, Lord. Yes. Are you? How embarrassing."

Eventually, the two reached the film company's front door. However, their knock went unanswered. They were not even sure they had the right address, given the strange dairy sign. ("Please compare our fresh-made butter with cold-storage goods other creameries are selling.") A moment later, though, a motor van came from behind the building and stopped at the curb.

"Are you here for our moving pictures?" the driver asked.

"It's acting, isn't it?" Estelle replied.

"Well, get in. We're off to Newark."

The driver said he was Charles Blanchard. The man in the back of the van identified himself as James Scanlon, the camera operator.

"Jimmy and I were expecting two fellows for you to act with, but since they seemed to have missed the ferry, we'll have to change our scenario," Charles said.

They arrived at the fairgrounds as the Benz was

being rolled out of its garage by the automobilist, Milford. Jimmy set up the Pathé camera and adjusted the film magazine. With the Benz firing its engine, Charles explained the scenario to his actresses. Margaret was to be Milford's daughter. Estelle was to play his wife. The story was that despite the pleas of the two women not to race, the driver vows to compete for the prize money to keep the bank from repossessing the family farm.

As prearranged, Milford drove the machine near the camera, then stopped so that Estelle and Margaret could pantomime great distress, begging their beloved not to race. Milford, in his goggles and leather racing helmet, his mechanician in the seat beside him, merely waved at the two women. For this, he received ten dollars.

Then, while the racing team prepared to get under way, the camera was repositioned by the distant turn from the bleachers to capture shots of the Benz approaching. Charles and Margaret remained with the press people near the garage, where drinks and food were being served. Estelle accompanied Jimmy to see the filming, curious about what the process involved. However, as the race car gained speed on its second lap, coming toward the camera, a tire apparently picked up a nail from the track, and a popping sound could be heard. The machine veered and shook, and all at once it tumbled violently down the track, twice going end over end. Hitting the inside fence, it was thrown high into the air, where Milford, his mechanician, and the machine were all separated in flight. The Benz landed on its nose in the muck of the pond that was at the track's center, not a hundred feet from the camera, its rear wheels sticking fully out of the water. Milford and his aide landed nearby and splashed about, apparently unhurt.

Jimmy had been filming the entire time, and he continued doing so, shouting to Estelle that he was certain he had gotten all the crash on film. Estelle, inspired by the excitement, said something had to be made of it. Thinking quickly, she suggested a scenario. The wife of the auto pilot, herself, would swim to his rescue. They could complete the story around the scene.

Jimmy thought it a great idea, so with no hesitation, Estelle jumped into the chilly water and swam toward the machine, with the crowd from the garage now running down the auto track. For whatever reason, Milford began to wave at Estelle as she swam, only enhancing the scene. When Estelle reached the dazed Milford, she found the pond was shallow enough for her to stand. She took his arm and they began to tread sluggishly through the mud toward the track and camera, the rescue appearing completely authentic.

When they got to shore, Milford embraced Estelle, mainly out of exhaustion, but it further improved the scene. The crowd had now reached them, and with his cuts and sprains innumerable, but with no apparent broken bones, Milford was taken by friends to Newark's emergency hospital. The mechanician, it was found, was completely unscratched in the ordeal.

When Charles was told the entire rescue had been filmed around Estelle's improvised story, he was ecstatic. Back at the studio, additional scenes were shot on the studio's outdoor set, with Estelle in dry clothes and Charles in goggles and leather helmet, playing Milford. Titles were written, shot, and spliced in, and in hours a one-reel epic – nine hundred and seventy feet of film, with a running time of thirteen minutes – was born, *The Racer of Newark Heights*. Charles said he planned to promote it for a week, then offer it to theatres.

For their labors, Estelle and Margaret each received five dollars and a ride in the Blanchard Brothers motor van to catch the five o'clock ferry to Manhattan.

"Can you come back Monday?" Charles asked, depositing them at the pier.

They nodded agreement.

"We'll provide box lunches every day, and in summer we'll pay an extra dollar because we'll be able to work later in the evening."

The next morning, a Saturday, the *New York Times*, which had had a man at the Newark track, ran a brief article with the headline, "Movies got this crash."

> Moving picture operators at the Newark Motordrome witnessed the unexpected yesterday, filming dramatic scenes that were very different from those anticipated. The New Jersey film company of Charles and Henry Blanchard, a new motion picture manufacturer with no released photoplays to date, captured a startling track accident.

The article speculated that the film might be able to document the cause of the mishap and that the American Automobile Association planned to send an official to the Blanchard Brothers studio to take possession of it.

> "The races on the track are sanctioned by the association, and we do not feel a moving picture of the unfortunate incident is suitable for audiences," a representative of the group said.

Arriving at the Fort Lee studio Monday morning, Estelle learned that Charles took the negative and decamped to a Manhattan hotel over the week-end, before the association officials could find him. He planned to place quarter-page ads in papers in New York, Philadelphia, Hartford, and Boston, saying the film would premiere immediately, "allowing anyone to see the sensational crash with no favoritism."

A federal judge did not heed the association's demand to stop the movie's distribution, and it was on screens, running continuously by Wednesday. At week's end, Charles would tell Estelle proudly that thanks to her efforts there were no unsold tickets at any theatre showing the film. He would offer her a salary of forty dollars a week, and he would also give orders that all auto races in Newark were henceforth to be filmed.

Acting was the sole ambition Estelle took from her tattered childhood. Her father had been the president of the bank in Billings, Montana, but when she was just a month old, he committed suicide, having squandered the bank's reserves on unwise ranch investments. Estelle's mother was left penniless. Unable to care for the child, she wrapped her in window curtains and left her on the steps of a foundling asylum.

A year later, still unadopted, Estelle was sent to St. Ambrose's, an orphanage in Helena run by Catholic nuns. One of the nuns, Sister Bernadette, was Canadian and had a theatrical bent. She adored the French actress Sarah Bernhardt, and she would stage religious plays each Saturday, often using her own scripts. Estelle fell under her tutelage, learning the fundamentals of drama and becoming the president of the Orphans' Theatre, which put on melodramas each Wednesday in the dining hall.

At seventeen, Estelle left the orphanage, having secured a job as a hotel chambermaid in Billings. However, she quit two weeks later, after winning a role in a musical revue passing through the town. She had claimed she was twenty-two. (Her mature face allowed her to play mothers and even grandmothers from the start of her career.) Owing to her fluency in French, she obtained a minor place in Bernhardt's company in 1906, on the actress' first farewell tour of the United States.

It was while on that tour in the Midwest that Estelle visited a nickelodeon for the first time. As a child, she had seen kinetoscopes, machines with peepholes and crank handles in which one would watch loops of film showing dancers and boxers. When she first heard the word "nickelodeon," she thought those machines were what people were talking about, because she had paid a nickel to view a line of them.

However, in Chicago one morning, she and another curious actress hired a taxi and asked to be taken to a nickelodeon. They were transported to a part of the city they would have avoided otherwise, a low-rent commercial district with an air of crimes freshly committed. The movie house had just been installed in a vacant barber shop. Painted in the front window was the sign "Grand Program of Dramatized Stories – No Show on Earth Like It." And here this building looked as though it was about to be demolished, Estelle observed. ("That's the picture business," her friend said. "Great talk about nothing.")

It was ten o'clock in the morning when the front door opened. The two purchased tickets and took their places on a bench, the first patrons inside. The air was rank, and a man came down the center aisle spraying perfume from an atomizer. The benches quickly filled with men and a few rough-looking women, some cradling babies. Many of the men were smoking pipes or cigars and talking loudly. Estelle heard less English than Italian and French.

The projection machine in the rear started with a sputter, and a beam of light illuminated the thick haze of smoke. Immediately, the crowd of perhaps two hundred people fell silent. The first photoplay, *The Accidental Hero*, was about a nearsighted man with an umbrella who foils a bank robbery by inadvertently poking the gun-toting robber in the eye. Estelle thought it embarrassing for the actors, but she began to watch the audience as much as the film. Once the moving picture started, there was complete silence. At first, she was sure they hated it and felt some vindication for the theatre, but then she looked around to see that people were gazing openmouthed, as if awestruck by what unfolded on the screen. When the film ended, there was wild applause.

The two women viewed an hour of such films. Estelle's friend left with the conviction that legitimate theatre would get no competition from movies ("Imagine *King Lear* done in ten minutes in silence"), but for Estelle something shifted about uneasily in her thinking. She kept recalling the expressions of utter wonder on faces in that audience. She had never witnessed that in the theatre.

2.

News hawker with a rumor

The rumor began to circulate in the early morning among the curb brokers in Manhattan's financial district that an aviator had taken off from New London, Connecticut, with the intent of flying through the lower part of New York City, through its canyons of skyscrapers, and then circling the Singer Tower. Sudden gusts barreled through the streets downtown, ricocheting unpredictably off the buildings, so the feat would certainly be among the greatest in flight history.

Bill Trowbridge was an aspiring actor who lived with Estelle in her apartment on 87th Street. He heard the rumor about the aviator after breakfast, when he went to the street to buy a newspaper. Estelle passed him on the sidewalk in silence – and, Bill knew, in anger – on her way to the New Jersey ferry. She was bound for another day of motion-picture work. The studio was also looking for actors, but Bill declined, upsetting Estelle with his reason. ("I'd lower myself by appearing in movies, as you will, too.") Bill first met Estelle at an audition the previous fall. She got a part; he did not, but fresh from vaudeville, he pressed her for advice about theatre, which became flattery that led to their romantic involvement. To deceive Estelle's landlord, who was anything but deceived, Bill posed as her brother.

Now, on the street, Bill listened to the story of the approaching aviator along with a crowd of similarly unshaven men, all purchasing papers. It was Saturday. A broker near Exchange Place told a passing chauffeur, who told their news hawker. The men excitedly got into the business of estimating the machine's flying speed, time of arrival, and path into the city.

"I bet it's the Hungarian, Egressy. He's the type to try it. He's been in the air races up at New London."

"You can't do it. You ever watch the flags on Second Avenue? Watch how they change direction every second. He'll be blown right down."

As if of a single mind, they began to move along the street in a group, talking of a likely building that would be open for rooftop viewing. The five strangers, drawn together like brothers by the spectacle, decided that the City Investing Building was the place to be, within sight of the Singer

Tower. They convinced a fellow in a passing motor to take them, and soon he, too, was caught up in their excitement.

A policeman on lower Broadway confirmed the rumor when they stopped for water for their machine. Yes, it was Egressy, flying his Burgess-Wright biplane, and he was headed for Hell Gate at the mouth of the East River. It was Egressy's stated intention, based on sources who telephoned the station house from various points on the route, to circle every tall building in lower Manhattan, a feat that was undeniable in its peril.

"Listen what he did," the policeman said. "He saw a train coming down from Bridgeport on the New York, New Haven, and Hartford, and so he decides to fly very low, within sight of anyone who bothered to look out their window, and he circled the train three times, passing right in front of the locomotive."

Atop the City Investing Building, to which they gained access by enlisting a janitor in the undertaking, they spread out along the roof's edge, a line of spotters. In loud voices meant to carry in the gusting wind, they introduced themselves for the first time: a bank clerk, a teacher, an actor, a stock-and-bond man, a druggist, another bank clerk, and a janitor.

Something seemed to sweep through them simultaneously, though. No more talking about careers. Here they were involved in something more elemental, something more about who they really were. This great adventure of aviation was what they, as men, were more aligned with in their souls. Life for a man was not acting or securities or prattling away to a classroom of students. It was up here, in the grasp of driven winds, with a view to all horizons, waiting for Egressy.

William Charles Trowbridge was born in 1886 in Boston, and at an early age he learned that relations with women amounted to a poker game in which he had been dealt a straight flush: his good looks. His first memorable experience of that sort came when he was thirteen. An Irishwoman in her forties with a notorious reputation (she could arrange abortions with some of the finest physicians of the city hospital) invited him into her bedroom, giving him two dollars afterward to keep quiet about it.

Bill's father had been a clerk at the Western Union office in Boston until he was fired for being drunk on the job. He then held a series of day labor jobs before moving his family to Providence, where the money came primarily from his wife's mother.

Young Bill, who inherited his father's dissolute ways, was a better-than-average student in school. However, a series of expulsions for a variety of offenses, including taking bets on boxing matches, landed him in strict Catholic schools, something that quickly turned him against education.

In his youth, Bill became intimately familiar with the criminal life of the city. When police shut down Providence's pool halls for running gambling books, eager boys like him were hired and sent out into the city's business offices, saloons, and cafes to collect bets from the poolroom regulars. Bill's best method of making money involved traveling to Boston and going around to mercantile houses dressed in his Sunday suit. He would tell people he was on his way from Philadelphia to Portland, Maine, and had lost his railroad ticket. He carried an official-looking letter on the stationery of the Industrial Department of the Waifs' and Newsboys' Home of Philadelphia. It identified the bearer as John Coughlin, who was being sent to live with his elder brother. It said that the boys' mother had recently died, leaving both sons as unfortunate orphans. On a typical day of such begging, Bill might collect ten dollars.

Under these influences, Bill's view of justice was that there were two sets of laws in America. There were the laws that made sense, such as those having to do with murder, rape, and other mistreatments of people. Then there were the laws to be winked at, most of which involved money, laws that were part of the social negotiation between the rich and the poor.

His reasoning was this: Rich men made the laws, and they made them to enrich themselves at the expense of the poor. Poor men committed petty crimes, and they did so to make themselves and their families less poor, a noble cause. As the poor had no means to make laws to enrich themselves, petty crimes would have to do.

His entrance into acting came when he was nineteen. He was working as a lifeguard at a beach near Providence and was asked to appear in a local summer production there, playing a lifeguard. Whistles from females in attendance convinced an actors' agent to sign him for vaudeville. For five years, he was half of "Ryder and Jones," an act that involved constant comical interruptions of Bill as he attempted to do magic tricks with playing cards. In 1910, bored with life on the road, he quit and moved to New York City, where he was having little luck until he met Estelle.

3.

A cab in the rain

With a cold drizzle falling, Estelle waited under her umbrella with Margaret Eagan at the ferry gate on the Manhattan pier. Bill was to meet her with a cab, but he was late. Finally, she saw a hat waving at her out the window of a horse-drawn taxi.

"I got into an argument with the cab wrangler," Bill explained as they got in. "I started to get in a motor taxi until he tells me what it costs. So I switched. I can't figure it. A horse has got to eat, so why should a motor cab cost four times as much?"

Estelle said they were giving Margaret a ride to her apartment on 101st Street. Once under way, Bill tried to describe the camaraderie that had developed that morning above New York, even though Egressy had failed to appear.

"The police finally made us come down when

someone called in a suicide report. They thought we were all about to jump," he said.

"A fellow did jump from the Singer Tower," Margaret said.

"Today? I would have seen him."

"No, yesterday. I read it in the *American*. He entered a musical score in a competition here in the city. A judge in Albany, after he finished with it, he mailed it back to New York, and somehow it got lost. The author was so upset that he took the leap. He said in the note he left that he didn't bother to write out a copy, he was so convinced God would protect it."

Since the cab ride began, Bill had been openly staring at Margaret, unable to disguise his interest from Estelle. Margaret seemed completely aware of it and played to it, flirting in an obvious manner. At the studio, Estelle had observed behavior by Margaret that was just as flagrant, especially toward Charles Blanchard, who had a wife and three children. However, she had to acknowledge that in a city that was a congress of beautiful women, Margaret would still be able to draw gazes on any crowded street.

Estelle told Bill that Margaret had been married five months to the day. "And, dear, didn't you say he's a playwright? A boy from a rich family?"

"His family is rich, but he isn't, I'm sorry to say. Our wedding money is already running out. He's been writing theatre reviews for one of the Bronx papers and that's all he's sold. You boys should be happy that Estelle and I are willing to work in movies. From what I hear, we've got the only wages in the group."

"Your husband's a writer," Estelle said. "Get him to write some film scenarios for us."

"Frank thinks it would be a waste of his time. He's a snob about theatre, I'm afraid. He doesn't think flickers will last. He thinks they'll be a fad like radium cures. And because they don't list the actors' names in the credits, he thinks there'll never be any fame in movies, so no money."

"Some are getting famous," Estelle said. "*Harper's* writes about them."

"I just worry both you women are making a mistake," Bill said. "You could lose your reputations. Dramatically, what can be expressed without speech?"

"First, I don't *have* a reputation," Margaret said. "Second, look at my expression, Bill. What am I expressing in regards to your opinion?"

She tightened her mouth and eyes in mock disapproval. Bill laughed loud enough that the driver turned.

To Estelle, Margaret was becoming a character in a bad play, a "type" whom the author describes in a few glib phrases in the script's first page. ("Young and beautiful; thinks the world revolves around her.")

Estelle would chide herself about forming such

shallow opinions of people, but if she saw no evidence to the contrary, then the opinion would soon settle into her thinking as fact. However, she feared that Bill soon would be reduced to just a line or two himself. ("A wandering eye, faithless, a Lothario.")

Estelle had been married briefly when she was nineteen, to an actor who was thirty-seven. As everyone warned her would happen, it did not last. Within a year, they separated. If nothing else, it relieved her of the desire to be married. She did not accumulate silver settings for her future husband's household or learn to shoot a rifle to be more appealing to a man. She harbored no illusions about marriage the way women did who had never experienced it. Her brief union told her the ideal of marriage was yet another example of the way life entices you forward with promises that cannot be kept. Bill was her first involvement in three years, and she was already wondering how long it would last.

At the audition where they met, Bill had entered the hall late, but instead of sitting with the mass of actors and actresses in the front rows, he had joined Estelle, who was sitting alone in the rear. He asked her for acting advice, saying he had only worked in vaudeville. There was something about their quiet, personal conversation that afternoon, carried on below the loud chatter of others in the hall, that had given her a sense they were perhaps a couple in the spiritual sense, "two who are one," as the song title said. Bill had remarked that no woman had ever spoken to him as honestly. ("Too many just like me for how I look," he said.)

Now, as the cab proceeded down Second Avenue, Margaret told a story about working several days for the Vitagraph studio in Brooklyn the previous fall. One morning, they were sent to an ice house with a scenario about an ice man delivering his goods on a hot day.

"The man who owned the ice house read in a newspaper that the Dix girl, the heiress who was abducted from her school in Pennsylvania, had been found alive in a motion-picture factory in Chicago, in the hands of kidnappers. I personally think she ran off to be in movies, but this ice house owner was so convinced I was kidnapped that he called the police. We wasted the whole day in the station house."

Bill, who had been continuing to gaze no less obviously at Margaret, said that he might give movies a chance, that Estelle was trying to get him to go over to New Jersey.

"So what do you think, Margaret? Would I look good on the silver sheet?"

She laughed then reached across and patted Bill's arm, a gesture that caused Estelle to look out the window as if distracted by the passing street life.

4.

Making up for a scene

Marion Fiske washed out a tub caked with spoiled butter, the stench forcing her to hold her breath periodically, as carpenters worked in other parts of the creamery, creating rooms and offices for the film studio.

Just seventeen, in her junior year of high school, Marion had no aspirations to act. Hired as a part-time seamstress in the afternoons by the Blanchards, she intended to enroll at the College of Saint Elizabeth in New Jersey to become a teacher like her mother. Her father had died in an industrial accident when she was three.

On her first day on the job, however, as she put collars on dresses, Charles Blanchard had rushed to the barn to find her, leading her by the hand to the outdoor set – three walls and a dirt floor – since they momentarily needed an actress. ("In this part, you faint away, just falling back into the chair, as the robber waves his pistol.")

Charles' brother Henry, who concerned himself mainly with the business of the studio and usually kept to his office, failed to advertise for professional actors the studio's first day, so even a visiting bottle salesman, who was not aware the creamery had closed, was enlisted as an actor. Marion did exactly as told and then was dismissed, but with an approving nod from Charles.

The following evening, as she prepared to leave, she passed a room in which a screening of the previous day's filming was being conducted by the Blanchards. She lingered behind the door, peering through the crack at the hinges.

When her scene appeared, Charles made the comment, "Now, that girl has a wonderful face, don't you think?"

Quiet and petite, Marion had recently begun to notice the attention boys were paying her in school. It was, she told her mother, as if her face had suddenly appeared that year after being absent all the other years. In some manner, she resented their inattention to her for so long.

Marion did not feel herself to have ambition in the usual sense. She had little interest in her school studies: Latin, medieval history, commercial accounting, geometry. What place would any of these things have in her life? She did not have dreams of a great career as so many girls did these days. She did not crave excitement or adventure or novel experiences. What she desired was to take long hot baths with a pint of lavender water added, wear white dresses, freshly starched and ironed, and spend hours in the kitchen cooking with her mother – which she enjoyed more than eating.

However, there was a standard in her thinking for what any moment of the day should be. On her back porch was a large beechwood rocker. Its creak as it rolled back and forth was nearly music to her. To be in that rocker on a June morning, pillows beneath and behind her, and to have the latest *Woman's Home Companion* or *House and Garden* in her lap was to experience perfection.

Later in her first week, Charles again called on her to act, this time playing the role of a lovesick shop girl. ("You're extremely shy and you refuse to look this strange fellow, who will be me, in the eye, but you smile. Can you do all that?" Charles asked her.) So in succeeding days, as she sewed or cleaned, she did so with an anticipation that she might be called in front of the camera at any moment. However, to her disappointment, another week had now passed and she had not been asked again, no doubt owing to the hiring of professional actresses and actors.

On this afternoon, she was assigned duties cleaning the butter processing room. She had been told to stay clear of the outside parking area, where two unwanted sheds on the grounds were to be burned down as part of a fire scenario. Charles told her the story was of a young woman rescued from a burning house by her long-lost mother, "to be played by the stage actress Estelle Harrison."

The sheds were now being dragged to the middle of the parking area to meet their fate. Marion saw the woman she assumed to be Estelle: tall, older-looking, her black hair in a bun. Marion's heart sank, though, when she saw Charles instructing a second woman, as young as herself and very beautiful. Evidently, she was a professional actress who would play the rescued daughter.

Minutes later, however, Charles yelled Marion's name, summoning her to the set. She was told to stand next to the second actress, who was introduced as Margaret. Then she was asked to cough as if inhaling smoke, to shake as if sobbing, and to pantomime a scream for help.

"Well, dear, you've got the part," Charles said. "There's now to be two sisters."

She was handed a torn costume dress and a bit of charcoal and directed to the one remaining shed to make up for the fire scene. Kept as a dressing room because it connected to the main building's water closet, the shed had one chair and one mirror hung on a bare wood wall. Marion streaked her face with the charcoal and mussed her hair, trying to keep her overall appearance dignified. She was preparing to step out of her own dress when Estelle walked in, opening the door to the view of several carpenters in the yard.

Estelle took the one chair, then opened her makeup case and began sorting through jars. She asked Marion what kind of experience she had as an actress.

"I've done only two things."

"Stock?" Estelle asked.

"What's stock?"

"What do you mean, what's stock?"

Flustered, Marion remained silent.

"Do you mean you don't know what a theatre stock company is? Exactly what two things have you done?"

"Well, they haven't thought up titles yet. They were pictures we worked on before you started," Marion said meekly.

Estelle's silence was a statement in itself. Marion quickly finished and left for the outdoor set. Later, as the camera was being positioned, she overheard Estelle tell a handsome younger man, who was apparently her husband, judging from their mutual familiarity, that "movies will go nowhere if untalented people can find any place in them." A chill ran through her.

Charles described the two scenes that were to take place. Marion and Margaret would be on the set, which had been made up as a parlor, smelling smoke and pantomiming anguish. Then Estelle would be filmed by the burning sheds, showing her anguish.

Oily rags were lit by the set, and Charles pushed the smoke into the parlor by waving a bed sheet. Marion began to panic. Here she was, about to act with professional actresses, and she knew nothing about acting. Nothing.

"Girls," Charles said as the camera began filming, "clutch each other as if in fright . . . Good. Margaret, you let out a scream, and Marion, you sob, dear, as you did for me; sob quietly as if resigned to your death . . . That's good . . . Margaret, clutch your sister."

When the camera stopped, Charles commended both women for their efforts. Then the sheds were set afire and allowed to reach full blaze. With the camera shooting and the burning sheds behind her, Estelle pantomimed great fear about entering the building, making grand gestures with her arms and clutching her bosom. Charles became frantic.

"What are you doing?" he yelled.

Estelle explained that was how one acts.

"My dear," Charles said, "you see no balcony here. There are no people hundreds of feet from the stage. The camera is right here. Please, less acting, and hurry!"

Afterward, in the dressing shed, preparing for the rescue scene, Estelle and Marion did not talk. The silence became so tense that Marion resolved to say something, anything, but it came out badly.

"You know, you're so much older and more experienced than me, sometimes I'd like to hear about all your stage experiences."

Estelle turned sharply. "How old do you think I am?"

"I only meant you've been acting longer."

With that, Marion knew they would never be friends.

Later in the afternoon, when Margaret and Estelle were sent to a location elsewhere for scenes, Marion was recruited from her cleaning duties to be the wife of a policeman played by the actor who, she thought, was Estelle's husband.

Charles called both over, saying to Marion, "We need you to act with Bill here. We also need a blue jacket for him. What size do you think he is?"

Bill playfully pushed his chest out, his wavy black hair glistening in the sun. Marion, her heart racing, thought she had never seen a man more striking in appearance.

While the camera was being set up, Bill remarked to Marion, "You tell me if I need to do something different. I haven't acted in front of a camera before."

"Just do nothing special. That's what I've found works best."

As if deferring to an experienced actress, Bill thanked her and introduced himself. Bill Trowbridge. From vaudeville and Boston. Marion Fiske. From Teaneck.

"Tell me, are you and Estelle married?" she asked.

5.

Hood's Theatre on Broadway

When eight films had been completed, the Blanchards made arrangements to hold their premiere at a theatre owned by a cousin, on Broadway near Union Square.

By this time, the company had learned the details of the brothers' background. Henry and Charles, in their early forties, had inherited their father's once lucrative string of hardware stores on Michigan's Upper Peninsula at a time when the profits were disappearing. Still in possession of the family riches, though, they had searched for a new investment and found the movies. As it happened, they had a cousin, Walter Hood, who recognized the nickelodeon craze early, and by the start of 1909, he had opened Hood's Theatres in two dozen cities in the East. Charles visited his cousin's movie house in Philadelphia while on a business trip there. He saw what a gold mine this inexpensive business was and how uncomplicated the one-reel films it showed were, reporting all this to his brother.

Henry, thin of face, taciturn, cynical in his view of people, was the businessman of the two, and his eyes fairly lit up when he saw money or any opportunity to make it. Charles, barrel-chested, an outdoorsman, an admirer of Teddy Roosevelt, had little interest in commerce. He had acted in his college days but was ordered, with the threat of the loss of his inheritance, to give up any stage ambitions and join the family business. So the idea of being in the motion-picture industry appealed to both brothers but for different reasons. Toward that end, they made the decision to move east, buying property for the studio and homes for their families in Fort Lee.

The Blanchards' cousin had intended his Broadway movie house to be his showplace theatre. He lavished money on it, fitting it with chandeliers and oil paintings in the lobby as well as cushioned seats and velvet wall coverings inside the main hall. However, none of the Blanchards' actors and actresses knew anything of its splendor before the premiere, with each holding the view that nickel theatres were only a step up from saloons and gambling dens.

On a Saturday evening, Estelle and Bill took a taxi down Broadway dressed in their best clothes.

They passed the legitimate theatres, where crowds filled the sidewalks. Estelle's embarrassment grew at the prospect of attending a nickelodeon in such finery. ("I hope it's been fumigated," she said with no humor in her voice.)

However, stopped in traffic north of Union Square, they could see crowds beneath the lit marquee of a theatre ahead. They also saw automobiles and carriages pulling up, delivering well-dressed men in top hats and women in furs, giving the appearance of any opening night on Broadway.

When they arrived, they found Charles in a tuxedo, welcoming the crowd in front and handing out printed commemorative booklets entitled "The New Age of Photoplays." He directed a white-gloved attendant to take Estelle and Bill inside. They were led to roped-off seats in the front row. A string quartet, surrounded by arrangements of flowers, was playing before the drawn curtain. Frank and Margaret Eagan soon joined them, as did Marion Fiske with her mother.

Almost as impressive to Estelle as the theatre's opulence was the audience's affluence. There was glittering jewelry everywhere she looked. The explanation, she found in talking to a couple behind her, was that Charles had given printed invitations to all the men at his Michigan Club in Manhattan. One card was shown to her.

"Have you never seen a motion picture? For your benefit, an exclusive presentation of this novel entertainment has been arranged at a fine new theatre on Broadway. See what has so strongly gripped the public's imagination. Evening dress is recommended," it read.

The lights dimmed and the brothers entered and stood by the quartet. At Charles' signal, the music stopped. Perhaps four hundred people now filled the room. He thanked them for coming and singled out notables in the audience, among them the city's mayor, William J. Gaynor. Heads turned to get a glimpse. Charles spoke of "man's inventive nature" and "the triumph of science." Then the brothers stepped aside, and the curtain opened to reveal the screen of stretched canvas. Soon the projection machine began to send flickering shafts of light across the room.

The first film on the bill, *The Fisherman's Odyssey*, was about a whaling crew lost in a storm and the survivors' struggle to find their way home. When Estelle wept on screen at the news that her son was among the missing, she heard a woman crying behind her. When the boy, played by Bill, washed up on shore, seemingly dead, and his fingers began to move in the sand, there was cheering. Estelle herself was moved by the scene.

The other films were shown, drawing enthusiastic applause as each ended. *The Raspberry Soda. Sunrise. The Walker Women.* When the two-hour program finished, the string quartet again assembled before the screen and played a waltz as the crowd filled the aisles to leave. Men began to recognize Estelle. She was asked for autographs and congratulated. An elderly woman in a fox fur clasped Bill's hands tightly. ("I'm so very glad you didn't drown, young man.")

Estelle was still dazed by the experience as she and Bill took a taxi home. Bill said he felt a newfound respect for movies. ("That's the future. Sure, you'll have cheap movie theatres, but there will be theatres like that for the better people.")

6.

Henry and Charles Blanchard

A reporter from the *Bergen County Tribune* visited the studio late one afternoon. In the idle time between scenes, he interviewed those who were present: Bill, Estelle, and Marion. The following Sunday, in the *Tribune*'s entertainment section, alongside advertisements for Schlitz beer in brown bottles ("Light can't spoil it") and Ford's Hygienic Ice, there was this brief article.

There has been a lot of activity on Linwood Avenue in Fort Lee where a new manufacturer of photoplays, the Blanchard Brothers Company, has set up shop. They have a group of players that will soon be familiar to you, as they will be making many of their moving pictures in our community. Greet them if you see them working on a street corner or in a park.

First among the players is Estelle Harrison, a premiere name of the New York stage. In some circles, she would be called a character actress. She has wonderful powers of mimicry and a wide range of ability, so she is well suited for films with their varied stories and settings. These players have nothing to say in the silent show, but in life, they have opinions to express. Estelle, who is bravely willing to risk a reputation as outspoken, will readily engage you on the political issues of the day. Asked about the suffrage, she notes that not too many years ago women were not permitted on the stage. She asks, "Is it not a better and more beautiful world that they are?" Most intelligent men would agree, I'm sure.

Then there is Billy Trowbridge, an 18-carat fellow for sure. He is an unmarried merrymaker, and he is as handsome as they come. So look out, you females. While I'm sure he has no ideal girl in mind, like most fellows, he will know the right one when he sees her. But Bill tells a good joke as well, so he is a regular with the boys. He hopes to row for a local club this summer. Look for him on the Hudson at dawn. In fine shape, he will be the one on the oars who is not breathing hard. Billy comes out of the vaude houses, and he is an easy sort of chap. He says with a wink, "If I read it in the papers, then I believe it."

Then there is Marion Fiske, as wide-eyed and simple-hearted a girl as you will meet – and so adorable! She is the ingenue of this group. Ask her a question about herself and she shies from you like a schoolgirl, all giggles and blushes. On film, she will be a gift, I am sure.

On reading it, Estelle was amused but Marion was furious. ("Giggle? I've never giggled in my life!") Bill bought a half dozen of the papers and pinned a copy of the item, with his section underlined, to the dressing room wall.

In the mornings, the company would assemble on the outdoor set to plan the day's schedule. Then, while preparations were made for the scenes, Margaret would knit in a sunny spot, Estelle would pore over the *New York Times*, and Marion, who had resigned from her high school to work full-time, would read magazines. Bill had the habit of going off in a corner of the lot with Charles – when Charles was sober – to box. Both would strip to the waist and don light gloves. The punching was not hard, but the footwork would exercise their legs and lungs, and it was clear they enjoyed the manly spectacle they presented.

Charles had come to New Jersey with a burgeoning drinking habit. All in the company were aware of it. Just six weeks into the studio's tenure, there were now many days when Charles did not work in the afternoons and took little part in the daily meetings, the gin on his breath often evident by noon. So Henry, an accountant at heart, increasingly determined the direction of the company's efforts. What he wanted in a scenario was the predictable, the tried and true, that which had most recently succeeded for Biograph, Thanhouser, or Vitagraph.

Estelle's opinion of moving pictures was improving and she was becoming ambitious with her story ideas. However, on hearing her scenarios, Henry would get a certain expression on his face, as if he had been forced to eat spoiled meat.

When Estelle proposed a story told from a dog's point of view, Henry called it "too experimental."

Estelle said, "I think it would sell more tickets than the picture we did . . ."

"We can't sell more tickets," Henry said. "There aren't any more tickets to sell. Do what I say and do what we've been doing. It fills the seats."

Estelle then told Henry a story she had heard. At Biograph, when D. W. Griffith first wanted to use close-up shots, "some fool there said no, because the audience will be shocked that these people don't have arms and legs."

When Henry heard the word "fool," his expression tightened and his eyes narrowed with a finality. Such negotiations had ended for good, she knew.

Around the set, Estelle began to notice that Marion would take any opportunity to talk to Bill, openly flirting with him even when Estelle was nearby. One day, Bill and Marion were sent to a boys' military academy in Trenton. The school had enough surplus Civil War uniforms for the students to stage mock battles, which they were preparing to do that day. A scenario about Gettysburg was prepared. Estelle had no role in the drama or any immediate need to be at the studio, but because of her growing suspicions, she went along.

While artillery cannons and horse-drawn wagons were assembling in a meadow, the three, along with Jimmy Scanlon, waited in the Ford. At one point, Marion was talking about set lighting, saying she did not like the harsh light when the sun got directly overhead, but that Henry would not let them wait it out.

"I know when I get older I'll have to be especially careful about lighting," Marion said, looking right at Bill. "Bad lighting shows all the wrinkles on you. I'm just glad I don't have to start worrying about that yet."

The conversation moved elsewhere, but Estelle was struck by the chilling expression of innocence on her face as she said it.

Their film that day, *The Bride of Battle*, about a nurse's love for a wounded soldier, became a surprise success for the studio, and Henry passed the word that Marion no longer had any seamstress duties and that she and Bill were to be paired in a series of hospital pictures.

7.

West Haverstraw Hotel

In early June of 1911, Henry gathered the company and told them that the Blanchard families were returning to Michigan for the summer, but that they were being sent to West Haverstraw, New York, up the Hudson River, to continue making movies during the interim at a hotel there. Meanwhile, workmen would remove part of the roof from the studio and replace it with glass panels so that filming could be done indoors during the coming winter.

Henry promised that all rooms and meals at the hotel would be paid for by the Blanchards, so the company made hurried arrangements to sublet apartments, an easy task with the road season ending and theatre people streaming back to New York City. Jimmy Scanlon would be in charge at the hotel, and the Blanchards' business manager,

Leo Krause, would remain in Fort Lee to see to the distribution of the movies.

Margaret convinced Henry to allow Frank to join the company as a scenarist and occasional actor, saying she could not be without her new husband for the summer. In truth, her reason had more to do with the guarantee of wages and expenses for the two of them. So the following Monday, with several trunks of undeveloped film, two trunks of costumes, and two Pathé Professional cameras, the Blanchard Brothers players set out to West Haverstraw in the studio motor van and the Ford.

The technical progress of the twentieth century had yet to reach West Haverstraw, a village of not quite three thousand people. Many of its farms were still without electricity or telephones, and its roads were largely unpaved.

The Swedish couple who owned the hotel, the Nystroms, made a living from it by advertising in New York City newspapers to draw the citybound up the Hudson River in summer. The hotel had two floors, eleven bedrooms, and a back lawn suitable for an outdoor set. Also, it was close to useful locations: the granite cliffs of the Hudson River, Buckberg Mountain, railroad depots, firehouses, factories, stores, parks, and cemeteries. The Blanchards rented the entire hotel through September.

The company arrived in West Haverstraw late in the evening. They took a supper of boiled meat and potatoes in the dining room, had coffee on the back porch, and wondered what would lie beyond the darkness when morning came. The women retired to the second floor, the men to rooms on the first. Frank and Margaret took the large front room, by the Nystroms. Although it was common knowledge that Estelle and Bill lived together in the city, Jimmy assigned them separate rooms a floor apart, although he whispered to Bill that a back staircase came out right by Estelle's door. Another room was set aside for chemical developing, and still another as a dressing room.

Just after dawn the next morning, they were awakened by explosions nearby. Bill went to investigate, thinking there might be a film in whatever was going on. It turned out to be a farmer down the road using dynamite cartridges to dig holes for new apple trees in his orchard. Bill convinced him to let them film a war movie around it, with the explosions serving as cannonballs striking the earth. The farmer became excited by the prospect, and once the camera arrived, he set off one charge and was about to set a second when the cartridge went off in his hand.

Jimmy was filming at the time, unsure how quickly the charge would explode. The farmer was thrown to the ground, where he rolled around in pain, with blood all over his clothes. They rushed him to a doctor, and although he lost a finger, his hand and its movement were saved.

That night, after all the film was developed, the company viewed a negative print of the scenes – in which blacks were whites and vice versa – in the dining room. They watched footage of Bill acting as if he had been shot, but then the scene of the farmer being maimed came on the screen. Mrs. Nystrom was watching with them. She did not know they had filmed the incident, and thought an actor was playing a part. While the company was respectfully silent, she commented at how authentic the scene seemed to be and how impressed she was by his realistic acting, saying that scene was one they should certainly use.

A discussion then began that set the tone and intention of their enterprises for the summer. How does one act to bring more realism to a scene? What gestures? What expressions? What lighting and story lines should be chosen? They decided to formulate rules. Margaret and Marion got up and acted out scenes, and the others criticized what was unrealistic, writing down guides for how they were going to act.

When the discussion turned to stories, Marion proposed one about a rich girl who is blind and living with her parents. She falls for a hired man who does chores around the house. He is kind to her and they talk often. However, her meddlesome mother overhears them and fires him because he is poor and she does not want her daughter to love a poor man. The girl is so brokenhearted, though, that she packs a bag and walks into town on her own to find him, calling his name.

"It would be a beautiful story of her wandering through the streets asking, 'Have you seen Anthony? Have you seen my Anthony?'"

"Very good, Marion. We'll do it tomorrow," Margaret said.

"I think I can do the girl," Marion said.

"Bill can play Anthony, and Estelle would be right for the mother," Margaret said. "She plays older women so well."

Margaret surely meant it as nothing but a compliment, but the others turned to Estelle, knowing it would not be taken that way. It was not. Estelle slowly got up to leave.

"No thanks. Someone else can do it," she said. "Bill, are you coming?"

Bill did not move. "I don't know. I think it's good casting. You do play mothers very well."

Estelle refused a second time, staring at Bill now, who looked only at his coffee cup, turning it slowly in the saucer.

"Who else here can play it, even with proper makeup?" Marion asked.

Estelle, a restrained fury in her eyes, turned and left. The others looked at one another uncertainly. After some whispered discussion, it was decided that the part of the mother would be changed to that of a father, and Frank would play him.

Soon the excited conversation resumed. More ideas for scenarios were thrown out. More coffee was ordered from the kitchen. It went on until well after midnight, the ideas coming more enthusiastically as the group gradually became aware that with Henry no longer there to habitually undermine their ideas, to thwart them, anything was possible.

8.

The hotel's outdoor set

The pattern of their days quickly became established. The company would rise at dawn and eat breakfast while planning the morning's efforts. Casting of parts would be coldly methodical, which even Estelle came to accept. ("Oh, she'd be right." "I could do that." "Margaret would be good for that.") Clear, sharp instincts, most often shared by all, a phenomenon of simultaneity, determined their decisions. Locations would then be scouted, props collected ("Could we borrow your terrier dog / grandfather clock / hay rake for one hour? We're movie people"), and rehearsals would be completed. Shooting would take place until noon, when everyone returned to the hotel for the midday meal. The afternoon would be a repeat of the morning. Filming also took place on the three-walled set the company had built on the back lawn, with muslin sheets arranged over the open top to filter the harsh sun. Then, in the evening, after a late meal, there would be conversation on the porch or screenings of films in the dining room.

Scenarios often had a life of their own. Once, the company hired a circus elephant for a jungle story. The circus was appearing in Haverstraw, where the film was shot. However, the elephant showed up wearing its performing headdress for that evening's show and the trainer would not remove it, saying she did not like to have it off. So the story was changed to be about an escaped circus elephant. The trainer was asked to direct the elephant down the street at a fast pace as they filmed, but the street was muddy and the elephant kept getting mired, finally falling over with a great splash. The story was changed again to be about an escaped circus elephant that proves to be justice for a bank robber, crushing him in her fall as he flees. A scene then had to be shot in which Bill robs a bank, but after the group made arrangements with a bank president to use the building, a fire was reported elsewhere in the town, in a dry-goods store. All fires were filmed regardless of need, and to take advantage of this one, the story was changed to be about an escaped circus elephant that becomes justice for a fleeing arsonist.

Within the company, alliances quickly formed. Marion and Margaret became good friends. Bill, anxious to learn the technical side of the business, fell in with Jimmy Scanlon, and Estelle became friendly with Frank Eagan.

Initially, Estelle felt sorry for Frank. It was evident who held the power in his marriage. The son of a Southern judge, Frank was educated, quiet, and unconventionally handsome. In Estelle's opinion, he married hastily. Margaret was probably the first beautiful girl who ever took an interest in him. However, Frank was well read, and he and Estelle spent many hours talking about books and the ideas one gained from them.

Three weeks into their tenure in West Haverstraw, rain washed out one day, and according to forecasts in the local sheet, it was poised to eliminate two more. Sarah Bernhardt was traveling again, in *Camille*, the French actress' second farewell tour of America, and she was in Pittsfield, Massachusetts, up in the Berkshire Hills, just eighty miles away. So Estelle organized a trip to see her. ("The sacred institution of Bernhardt. It is an obligation, like climbing to the top of the Statue of Liberty, to experience it once in your life.") The plan was to take a morning train from Haverstraw, find a hotel, see the performance, and then come back by train the next morning.

They arrived in Pittsfield, found rooms in the Esquire House, and walked as a group to the

Colonial Theatre. Getting there well before the curtain, Estelle found the manager and told him they were a film company, Blanchard Brothers, up from New York for the performance, and that she had traveled on tour with Sarah and wished to visit with her afterward. The manager insisted on meeting the rest of the company, and he showed marked excitement as he shook hands with each of them, something Estelle could not explain. Was Pittsfield so small that even obscure movie players were celebrities?

The lights dimmed, the audience quieted respectfully, and the production began. To Estelle, it was vintage Sarah. Nothing had changed. She would give audiences exactly what they wanted and what they knew to expect. With the final curtain, the company waited for the theatre to clear, then the theatre manager arrived to escort them backstage. Coming into an open area adjoining the dressing rooms, they encountered a crowd of people. Heads turned. At first, Estelle thought all the attention was for Bernhardt. However, the manager, in a booming voice, announced they were the Blanchard Brothers movie players visiting Pittsfield, adding that the city was "blessed to have so much talent under one roof at one time."

A cheer went up. The manager then told Estelle that a program of Blanchard Brothers pictures, including *The Bride of Battle*, was playing just down the street at a Hood's Theatre, opened just a month earlier.

Estelle saw Sarah across the room now and pushed through the crowd toward her. From their year on tour, Estelle knew that Bernhardt hated everything about film actors. As Estelle approached, she prepared her explanation of why she had become one of them.

Sarah, recognizing Estelle, offered her hand then pulled Estelle close, whispering in her ear, "*N'as-tu pas honte?*" Have you no shame?

Having expected something pleasant and cheerful, Estelle felt a shiver of revulsion. Sarah soon returned to her dressing room, but the crowd stayed around the Blanchard Brothers people, peppering them with questions. The attention began to focus on Bill and Marion because of their roles in *The Bride of Battle*. Marion suggested that she and Bill embrace for the news photographer "as if I just found him alive in the field hospital." At that moment, Estelle fully understood Marion's intentions. Arriving back at the hotel, she confronted Bill about it.

"She's no more than the wardrobe mistress."

"She's an actress now. You have to give her credit. I was only a lifeguard. Now I'm an actor. We were all something before."

"She's no one. She doesn't deserve . . ."

"Then I don't deserve anything, either."

Estelle stopped, thinking that she was putting the seed of the thing into Bill's thinking, aligning him with the girl.

The next afternoon, back in West Haverstraw, if Estelle had retained any doubts about Marion, they were dispelled. The company hired the hose wagon of the Haverstraw Fire Department for a scene. It was to come flying down the street. Jimmy built a bonfire in an open lot so that the flames and drifting smoke would be in the corner of the shot as the fire wagon came toward the camera. There were no actors in the shot, but the company turned out to watch, with the exception of Bill, who went to a barbershop.

Even though all in the neighborhood had been warned that the wagon would be coming, a little Italian boy ran into the path of the horses and was trampled. Everyone rushed to the child. Estelle found herself standing next to Marion when the police ambulance arrived. With the boy's mother crying, a doctor examined the injured child, who was unconscious. Estelle heard Marion whispering to Frank, catching only partial sentences – ". . . an immigrant . . . Parents should teach children . . . His fault."

Then Bill arrived and Estelle watched as Marion's demeanor changed entirely. Cruelty suddenly became compassion. ("Poor child, poor, poor thing.") As if it were Marion suffering, Bill put a comforting arm around her and she pressed close to him.

The boy did recover, suffering only a broken

arm and a bad headache, so at that moment the lasting injuries were to Estelle, who knew what was about to be lost in her life. Bill's visits to her room at night were already growing infrequent. Estelle had issued a special invitation to him that day after breakfast, and when she did not hear his knock by midnight, she knew she would never hear it again.

9.

Haverstraw Station

Frank proposed the scenario for *The Celebrated Mr. Ames* at breakfast. It would be about a train conductor who foils a robbery, earning himself a large reward from the railroad. It would end with a woman passenger, a secret love of the conductor, to whom he has never mustered the courage to speak, giving him an inviting glance as he helps her from the train.

From the expressions about the room, this was not to be their marquee picture of the week. When it came time to cast it, Bill volunteered for the conductor, and when Frank characterized the passenger as "young and sweet," Margaret immediately suggested Marion. The company quickly moved on to a second story about survivors of a flood, suggested by Margaret. She and Estelle, with Jimmy Scanlon, set about forming that story.

Frank, Bill, and Marion took the Ford coupe

and a camera and traveled to the Haverstraw station. The day was hot and the road dusty. Bill sang an Irish ballad. Frank, who had become interested in directing, talked through the various camera shots as he drove. When they reached the depot, arrangements were made with the station master to shoot by a train on a side rail as it took on water. The robbery scene was shot alongside an empty passenger car, with Frank in a bandanna as the robber, Bill in a borrowed conductor's hat, and Marion cranking the Pathé. (By then every company member had learned the art of maintaining a steady two turns per second on the camera.) Frank positioned the camera by the car's steps for the final scene of Marion's inviting glance at the heroic conductor.

"Do I understand that at this point in the story the conductor has already received his reward money from the railroad company for halting the robbery?" Marion asked.

"Yes," Frank said.

"He's received his reward and this girl is aware of that, and she suddenly shows interest in him. Well, goodness. I would think the audience would think she's only interested in his money."

Frank stopped and considered this.

"You're right. I would, too," Bill said.

"Why not this?" Marion said. "She shows interest in him all along, but he's too shy to see it. She wants him to be interested in her, always saying some little thing to him, showing him attention. But then, at the end, after he's a hero, one more bit of attention like all the rest wouldn't really make sense. It has to be something more. Perhaps a kiss."

She surprised even herself with the idea, and all three mulled this over as the grasshoppers droned around them and the dust by the tracks lifted in a breeze.

"That might work," Bill said. "But it can't be just a little thing, a gesture. She has to be telling him she loves him."

Frank now seemed convinced of the need for changes, of the potential misinterpretation by the audience otherwise. He and Bill fell into a technical discussion of the kiss, of how it would proceed, as if they were talking about the workings of an automobile engine. Marion could bend her head to her left side, a thirty-degree angle, putting her right arm about his waist to signify willingness. Bill could remove his hat – no, tilt it slightly – no, remove it would be better – bending his head to his left, closing his eyes, his right foot a shoe length forward .

Marion tried to listen, but picturing the kiss now, her heart began to beat rapidly. She glanced over at Bill, who glanced back with something in his eye that said he, too, was thinking about this as more than acting.

Their movies often featured kisses, nearly

always as an ending – the melodrama relieved. Four times Marion had been called on to kiss Frank, twice as brother and twice as father. Only once had she kissed Bill on screen, and that came on a field filled with smoke, cannon fire, and military students running about in *The Bride of Battle*. She had no recollection of it, occurring as it did in high confusion. Now there would be this kiss, a considered kiss, one whose content of emotions and meaning she and Bill were both contemplating.

It was decided the scene would be shot behind the locomotive. ("No nice girl would kiss someone in front of a crowd.") Frank, immersed in the mechanics of the scene, positioned the Pathé and physically set Bill and Marion to reduce shadows. Marion grew only more anxious, nearly unable to breathe through this delay. Frank called for action. Bill pantomimed his lines and Marion replied. Then Bill removed his cap and leaned his head forward. Her heart racing, a boldness and calm suddenly overtaking her, Marion kissed him full-mouthed, not to the side as was the method on stage.

Frank, still concerned about technicalities, ordered a second shot of the kiss, telling Bill to approach her so that his profile could be seen more clearly. Marion delivered the kiss in exactly the same manner, and as they pulled apart, staying in her character, she leveled a gaze at Bill that said he should not miss the intention of the kiss. Frank, apparently seeing none of these subtleties, said he was satisfied with the shot.

Bill, Marion, and Frank ate dinner alone that evening. The others had stopped at a roadhouse when their filming was prolonged. During the meal, Frank talked about new story ideas he was developing, while Bill and Marion were conspicuously quiet.

Later, Bill and Marion sat by themselves and talked in whispers on the outdoor set. In a tree nearby, katydids droned and cows on a neighboring farm could be heard lowing. The air was rich with the aromas issuing from the Nystroms' rose garden. It was sometime after midnight when Marion, in possession of a package of "French preventatives," which her mother had obtained for her and ordered her to pack, delicately went down the hotel's back stairwell to Bill's door. She returned to her room before dawn, doing it so quietly that not even Bill was aware she had left his bed.

In succeeding days, the amount of time Bill and Marion spent together, and their undisguised attentions toward each other, made it clear to the others what was happening. The rumors were confirmed by the almost complete withdrawal from group meals by Estelle.

The hotel's thin plaster walls hid little noise late at night, and the subject of creaking bedsprings on the first floor, where not only Bill's room was but where Margaret and Frank and the Nystroms also had rooms, erupted into jokes one morning at breakfast. The laughing and humor brought Bill and Marion's affair into the light, an approving light that, by the meal's end, had officially rendered them a couple within the company.

Through July and August, the filmmaking continued, and every Friday, four or five edited one-reel motion pictures were placed on the noon train out of Haverstraw. Estelle cooperated as much as was needed, taking on a noble attitude even when asked to act with Bill or Marion. However, by August, she was staying in her room any time a camera was not cranking.

In September, with just two more weeks in their stay, Estelle got permission from Jimmy to leave early, saying she had a family emergency, despite the knowledge common to the company that she had no remaining family. It was assumed she went back to her Manhattan apartment.

By this time, through Marion's coaxing, Bill had agreed to marriage, and Marion convinced him to have the ceremony at the hotel – but as a surprise. A week before they were to return to Fort Lee, she told the rest of the company she had a scenario for a wedding story. She asked Jimmy to prepare the set for a church, Mrs. Nystrom to bake a cake, and a local minister to act what he thought would be a role in the story. Bill had no love of priests or the Catholic Church and agreed to a Presbyterian service. Marion stayed up much of the night before the ceremony, fashioning her wedding dress out of costumes.

Only when everyone was on the set following breakfast did Marion tell them the scene would be for real. The Nystroms were so excited by the prospect, they convinced Marion to wait two hours so that others in the surrounding towns who had come to know the company that summer could attend. By ten o'clock, the set overflowed with guests: firemen, policemen, a grocer, an iceman, a coalman, a baker, even an undertaker, as well as more than a dozen of their children, who did somersaults and cartwheels on the lawn until the ceremony finally got under way. Also among the gathered was a reporter from the *Haverstraw Times* who reported the event this way:

Wedded in West Haverstraw
Actress Marries Actor

Two featured players of the Blanchard Brothers motion picture company, which has been making its product in Rockland County this summer, surprised their fellows yesterday and became off the screen what they were playing on screen, which is to say newlyweds.

The actress Marion Dawes Fiske was married to William Charles Trowbridge at the West Haverstraw Hotel on an outdoor movie set splendidly arranged as a church. To this observer, it could have passed for the actual thing. The assembled were told only at the last minute that the ceremony was not to be a fiction for the movie houses.

The set was elaborately decorated for its purpose. Lilies surrounded the faux altar. The bride was gowned in white satin, her tulle veil caught up in a coronet of roses. Music was provided by the violin of Henry Nichols, Haverstraw councilman.

At the hour appointed, the Rev. Thomas Woods of the First Presbyterian Church performed the ceremony before about 60 assembled guests. Owing to the surprise of the event, no family members of either of the principals were able to attend. Margaret Eagan was the bride's maid of honor. James J. Scanlon was the groom's best man.

The bride and groom planned a short bridal trip to New York City today, where they are booked into the Plaza Hotel. The couple, who will make their home in Fort Lee, N.J., found their waiting motor decorated with white ribbons and quantities of useful household utensils. It also bore a placard with the inscription, "We Are Forever Married. Pity us."

10.

The newlyweds' cottage

Loaded down with cameras, costumes, luggage, and the depleted company, the motor van arrived at the studio late on Monday afternoon.

Bill and Marion, fresh from their honeymoon, smiling sheepishly, were already there but locked out. Jimmy produced the key. Inside, they found the new indoor set awash in light under a gleaming glass ceiling. They also found the business manager, Leo Krause, asleep in his office.

They had expected Henry Blanchard to be there, but they learned he had been delayed in Buffalo by a trainmen's strike. Charles, they were informed, was in an alcoholics' sanitarium.

Examining the set, they came upon what they initially thought was a canvas sandbag, part of some system for raising and lowering backdrops perhaps. However, Bill discovered that it was in fact a mailbag stuffed with fan letters.

For the hour until Henry arrived, they sat on prop furniture and read through them, reciting to one another the most glowing sentiments or most adoring phrases, the next more startling than the last. Several contained marriage proposals. Out of one, a ten-dollar bill fell, prepayment by the Brothers of Commerce in Watertown, New York, for a train ticket for Margaret to attend the Ice Glen Festival there as its queen.

Bill and Marion already were aware of the reputation their West Haverstraw films had gained. They told of running into an actor from Vitagraph outside the Plaza and of all the compliments he heaped on their efforts.

They were finally interrupted by Leo, who, organizing the storage lockers in the old barn, had not been aware they had opened the bags. He admonished them like children. ("Put every letter back in the bags! Now! Go wait outside! Now please!")

Later, after Henry got to the studio, Marion heard him yelling at Leo in his office, saying no actor should have seen those letters. ("They should have been burned, damn it!")

They soon learned the reason for Henry's reaction. The next morning, Leo requested to meet with the company in the screening room. As they assembled, Frank joked that they were about to be fired, that first-class actors and actresses were to be hired now that things were succeeding.

Leo's speech was short. "Henry and Charles are extremely grateful that their films are finally showing signs of making a profit, and with that in mind, they want to express their gratitude to you in the form of an offer of a contract that will guarantee you a weekly salary of ninety dollars for the next year."

Then he gave them the written contracts to look over and left. As everyone read, Margaret began to do some calculations, saying she suspected other motives on the part of the Blanchards. She got pencil and paper and figured just what level of profit the films were making based on what she knew of commercial rents, overhead, average attendance, and ticket prices. She calculated that the profits were huge, and she told everyone so. She also calculated that the brothers were intent on getting everyone under contract so that when they found out how popular they and the Blanchards' movies were becoming, they could not make the financial demands so common to stage performers whose stars were on the ascent.

Marion and Bill said they wanted to sign anyway. Estelle was uncertain. However, Margaret said she and Frank would refuse. This apparently surprised Frank, but he offered no opposition. It was decided to let Margaret have her say with Leo before anyone else made their answer known.

When he returned, Margaret rose.

"I don't think this is enough. Frank and I, we've been thinking about things, and we want one hundred and thirty dollars," she said.

"A week?"

"Now look. I know what's happening. I was up to a Hood's Theatre this summer in Poughkeepsie. I saw the crowds there. I saw the tickets selling. I know how much money the brothers are making. You tell them I want one hundred thirty a week and so does Frank. It's only fair. I'm a star and Frank writes and directs the movies that are making them rich."

Leo appeared astonished. "Is this how everyone feels?"

"We all agree the films are making a lot of money," Estelle said. "This isn't fair and I think you know it."

Henry had not yet come into work, so Leo had to call him at home. The company was silent as they strained to hear Leo's end of the conversation in the office next door. In a series of negotiations that involved Leo going back and forth to his telephone, the offer to all was increased to one hundred and fifteen dollars. All accepted. Later, they would find out Henry had wanted to fire all of them, but Leo advised him not to for the very reason that Margaret had guessed. The actors and actresses were becoming true stars of the silver sheet, and the company was making money hand over fist because of it.

Before returning to Fort Lee, Bill and Marion made arrangements to rent a house just five blocks from the studio. While they continued to stay at the Plaza, the home's interior was repainted and furnishings were purchased with the help of a professional decorator.

The furniture was delivered and placed on a morning when Marion was at work. At noon, a message was passed to her that the home was ready and the door keys would be in the letter box. Unable to stand the anticipation, she skipped her lunch and walked up Linwood Avenue. When she opened the front door, the sight took away her breath. Was this actually hers? A stack of delivery slips for tables, chairs, and other items lay in the kitchen. She carried them about the house, matching them to what she found.

In the last room she entered, the master bedroom on the second floor, there were satin sheets on the bed. Removing her shoes, she slipped between the glistening sheets and was overwhelmed by the bliss of the newlywed, something she had not felt at the crowded and noisy Plaza.

A monarch butterfly had come in through the open window on an idle autumn breeze. She watched now as it examined the ceiling by lightly bumping against it here and there before managing to find its way out the same window. She asked herself, could her contentment be any greater?

In August, while the company was still in West Haverstraw, the Blanchards reissued *The Bride of Battle* with the cast identified in the credits for the first time. They hoped to take advantage of the growing popularity of the actors and actresses that was being created by the new magazines devoted solely to motion pictures and their stars. The film gained a new life.

Once back in Fort Lee, Henry asked Bill and Marion to make a personal appearance at a new Hood's Theatre in Freehold, about fifty miles to the south, which was playing the picture. They would briefly address the audience before the film's first showing of the day.

On a Saturday morning, Bill and Marion boarded a train and took seats in a crowded car. Across the aisle from them was a young girl traveling with her mother. She was reading *Photoplay* magazine and at some point began to stare at Bill and Marion in an exaggerated way. Marion at first thought her touched, but then the mother and daughter began to whisper and the mother prodded the girl forward into the aisle.

"Are you them?" she asked Marion, pointing to the magazine.

Marion took hold of it. The Blanchards had

placed an advertisement in the issue for *The Lost Telegram*, in which Bill and Marion were also featured. It was one of the last movies filmed in West Haverstraw before their return to New Jersey. The advertisement included photographs of them.

With delight, Marion showed it to Bill and admitted to the girl that they were indeed that couple. The girl's excitement drew the attention of others in the car, and soon they were signing any available scrap of paper. For the first time, they felt the fame being cast on movie players.

When they got to the Freehold stop, they realized that others who had not been scheduled to get off there were following them from the depot, so that a small crowd stretched out behind them as they walked to East Main Street and the theatre. They turned the final corner to see a mob of nearly a thousand people crowded outside the theatre, with police officers struggling to keep order.

The moment they were recognized, there were screams and much of the crowd rushed toward them. They were quickly enveloped. Marion felt hands grabbing at her, and Bill pulled her in protectively, demanding that people move away. Four police officers got around them and rushed them, as best they could, to the theatre doors.

After order was restored outside, discussions went on inside about how to avoid a riot. It was decided that four hundred ticket buyers would be allowed in, and then Bill and Marion would appear in front of the screen and make their speeches. Marion, who had never spoken to more people at once than could fill a parlor, now felt she would faint as she waited.

Wild cheering broke out in the hall as Bill and Marion stepped before the screen. Marion had to begin her speech three times before it quieted enough that she could be heard. Nervously, but with a confidence that surprised her, she thanked them for coming, then talked about her character in the film, saying that she learns to "put love above all else." Bill said that as an actor he always endeavored to serve the story as best he could. When they finished, there was again wild, unrestrained applause, which they could still hear as they exited the theatre's back door. They left through an alley in borrowed hats. A police officer drove them to the next station up the line to catch the train back to Fort Lee.

Bill reported to Henry that he enjoyed the experience, but Marion refused ever to repeat it. ("It was like animals smelling carrion on the wind," she said.)

At home, Marion cleaned and cooked and felt a domestic quality rise in her. She also felt her ambitions as an actress disappearing. She found going to the studio to be drudgery no matter what the picture, especially when Bill would be sent out for location shots without her.

Once, she went to Henry and asked him specifically not to pair Bill and Estelle. He did not answer at first but then brought himself up in his chair.

"What is good for the picture is what I'll do every time, dear. If Estelle and Bill are right for a story, then they'll be placed in the story."

Marion, in a challenging tone, responded, "That's not going to please me. Not at all."

Over the next week, Marion got no starring role, and Bill and Estelle were made leads of a film about a time traveler who goes back to rescue his first love before she dies in an automobile accident. Marion spoke to Henry only when forced to from then on.

Filled by his growing notoriety (a *New York Herald* article referred to him as "the handsomest man in pictures"), Bill wanted to go into the city on weekends to find a party or to gamble illegally in clubs. Though Marion was willing to join him at first, she began to resist, saying she felt sickly or that projects needed to be done around the house.

At some parties, Marion would find a closed door in the apartment. Opening it, she would see people lounging on beds and on the floor, obviously taking cocaine or opium. However, it was blackjack and alcohol that Marion most feared on Bill's behalf, as it was these habits that he indulged. She knew she could push him only so far, though, before he would react badly. She began to anyway and finally refused to go with him into the city. He went by himself, often returning drunk.

Once, he brought back a seaman who had escaped from a navy prison ship in New York Harbor. He had removed his porthole bars and swum ashore. They arrived after midnight, both inebriated, and then sat in the kitchen drinking coffee.

Bill said, "Why, isn't this something, Marion? Schulte here jumped his ship. He's a wanted man."

Some nights, Bill would be dropped off drunk at the front door, just pushed out of someone's machine onto the lawn. Marion feared he would pass out and freeze to death. Often, she would cry late at night in the bathroom, feeling a misery she had not thought possible as a wife. She began to call in sick frequently to the studio. When it happened three times in a week, Henry, meeting with the company, asked Bill where Marion was. Bill told her about the conversation that night.

"Henry says to me, 'What have you done to our girl, Bill? Is there a baby on the way?' Then he swats me on the back in a congratulatory way. Except everyone else knows the truth, which is that you've decided you're upset at me and so you're refusing to work. So now they're all angry at me. They think I'm threatening their livelihoods by doing things that keep you home. So, damn it, Marion, quit acting like a baby about things."

11.

New Year's Eve, 1911

The line between 1911 and 1912 was passed on the streets of New York City in elegant bedlam. From 14th Street north along Broadway for nearly a mile, crowds filled the street by dusk, with a particularly large swell occurring near an electric sign on 21st Street that would announce when the new year had arrived in various world cities: Moscow, Stockholm, Paris, London. The obligatory cheers and eruption of horns and cowbells would follow instantaneously with each flash.

As a group, Bill, Marion, Frank, and Margaret walked over to Broadway from Third Avenue, where they had dined. The men wore tuxedos, the women gowns – all working clothes from various shows and productions, faint stains of greasepaint evident on several.

A light rain fell and the slush of day-old snow filled the streets, but the temperature was bearable. They stopped at the Wilcox Hotel near Times Square to drink champagne and toast the new year.

Through the evening, the din along Broadway rose as the hours of 1911 diminished. Ambitious hotel parties, by reservation only, spilled into the street near midnight with finely dressed revelers relating the details of their celebrations. One hotel stationed flower girls in the galleries to throw roses on the diners. Another handed out baskets woven of candy and presented diners with bronze statues of Winged Victory mounted on marble. Another had a sixty-piece orchestra, and all the women wore red leather masks.

Near midnight on their portion of the Great White Way, printed copies of Tennyson's "Ring Out, Wild Bells" were passed out to the crowd. All who had pocket watches held them aloft. Six minutes to go.

"Look here. This is wrong," Frank said, brandishing his Tennyson. "They wrote it out wrong: 'Ring in the noble modes of life.' It's 'nobler modes of life,' not 'noble.'"

"Oh, shut up," Bill said, his mild drunkenness making his intentions only friendly. He even threw an arm around Frank.

"It's wrong, though."

"Recite the Lord's Prayer without an error. Go ahead," Bill said.

"I could do it."

"Nine out of ten can't. So who cares about Tennyson?"

Midnight arrived and the noise grew louder and wilder still. Cheeks were bussed, flirtatious kisses were given, men's hands foraged beneath women's frocks – all of it lost in the elation of the crowd and then in the unexpected, unified movement up Broadway. It was as if those at the head of the crowd knew of a better destination, perhaps a hotel party open to anyone, and everyone else trusted that they did.

Church services along Broadway began promptly at midnight with the singing of psalms, but the raucous noise outside drowned out the harmonious sounds inside. Within the churches, those on the street were surely perceived as blasphemous drunks, the lost souls of the new century. On the streets, those in the churches, some of whom came to the oaken front doors to scold, were surely seen as pious and comical, people still mired in the last century.

Sleet fell steadily in New Jersey the morning following New Year's Day. Margaret and Bill were sent to Newark for a story about a woman whose personality changed when she put on different hats. Two extras, young women from the staff of a millinery store that Henry had made arrangements to use, stood with Bill beneath the shop's tin awning. Margaret and Jimmy waited with the camera in the Ford across the street.

Bill was telling the young women of his intended method of achieving wealth in the world, with the purpose of impressing one of them whom he thought a particular beauty – obviously Irish, with red hair and the lilt of the Green Isle in her voice.

"You would have to patent something critical to a process," he said. "That way – say your process is movies – that way people would have to come to you to make them. You'd get a royalty."

"So is it movies you have in mind?" asked the girl his eye was on. She turned slightly and her hatpin grazed Bill's shirt, prompting apologies between the two. ("I was too close." "No, I was." "No, certainly I was.")

"In fact, it's flying," he said. "It has to do with flying. I read somewhere a Frenchman got eleven passengers up in his monoplane. The combined weight was more than a ton, but he kept it up in the air for two miles."

"They must have been small people to get inside the thing," said the girl he did not have his eye on, who was shorter than her friend, her body lost in an oversized coat. She apparently had grown aware of Bill's disinterest in her and seemed to resent him for it.

"Well, it beat the old record of seven passengers. What this tells me is that someone is going to have the idea to start an air transport service."

"And?" said the shorter girl.

"And I plan to take out papers to . . . well, papers or maybe permits or official licenses. Whatever is needed in a territory. Then, when it dawns on people this is possible, to transport people around by air, the way trains do on the ground but faster, they'd have to come to me and buy out my license in order to operate in that territory."

"Why wouldn't these people just get their own flying license?" said the shorter girl derisively. "It doesn't make sense."

Hearing an approaching automobile backfire, the girl with the hatpin turned suddenly, and this time the sharp point scraped Bill across the cheek, drawing blood in a thin, beaded line. It caused more anguish in the girl than in Bill, who smiled at her great concern. She took out a handkerchief and dabbed repeatedly at his cheek, telling him over and over how sorry she was. Shortly, her comforting, her pressing against him, her dabbing and stroking began to be the manifestations of arousal, and soon, under the pretense of accepting her comforting, Bill pulled her close to him and they whispered apologies and acceptances of apologies as if they were lovers' murmurings.

This appalled the other girl, who turned away from them, shaking her head. The sleet suddenly intensified, loudly pelting the tin awning above them. After some whispering, Bill followed the girl into the millinery shop. She told her friend they were going for antiseptic. They disappeared for nearly an hour, not returning until the weather had cleared.

12.

Broadway friends

After fleeing West Haverstraw in her unhappy state the previous fall, Estelle looked up old friends from the stage once back in Manhattan. It was her intention to quit the movies and return to the theatre the moment her film contract ended, but it was a lean season in the play world and bookings were lacking. She listened to tales of distress, of Broadway shows closing in days and of touring companies disbanding on the road. Estelle kept quiet about her own good fortune.

She went to a party one afternoon at the 89th Street apartment of Annabel White, a stage actress she knew. Her husband, who had been manager at the Hudson Theatre, was selling suits at Macy's and Annabel was sewing at home, doing piecework between auditions. Estelle still knew most of their crowd, mainly struggling actors, but when she walked in the door, she felt an immediate chill.

Coincidentally, there had just been an article in *Motion Picture Story Magazine* about the rise of Blanchard Brothers, about the excellence of the studio's films, with photos of the company members and other press agentry material. Annabel had a copy, which she had shown about before Estelle arrived. ("We expected you'd be wearing diamonds and furs," someone commented.)

Later, they gathered around the piano to sing. A musical at the Winter Garden had a song, "Queen of the Dance Halls," which had become popular. Annabel started playing it and making up words.

There was a line, "If only I could dance, I'd be the queen of the Second Avenue ballroom. It's the finest show on Earth." Annabel turned to Estelle and sang right at her, "If only I could act, I'd be queen of the nickel show. It's the cheapest show on Earth."

Laughter exploded around the piano. Annabel, though, continued to gaze right at Estelle, not laughing, as if to say, "There, you've got what's coming to you."

Estelle returned home that night, vowing to remain at Blanchard Brothers, to work harder than ever in films, to forget about the stage, and to wring any success possible from motion pictures, as if to say to Annabel's crowd, "There, you've got what's coming to you."

The spring of 1912 continued to be lean for

stage actors and actresses. However, Sarah Bernhardt had made *Camille* as a film, earning thirty thousand dollars. It was so hugely popular that many in the theatre were turning to movies. The great Bernhardt had crossed the footlights. Movies had been baptized.

One evening, Estelle received a call from Annabel. She and her husband, both out of work, were about to lose their apartment, unable to pay the rent.

"I read about your salary in *Movie News*," Annabel said. "Is it true? Are you getting that much? Congratulations if you are. You deserve it."

Estelle was silent, but Annabel, apparently on a mission, pushed ahead.

"Look, Estelle. We've been friends how long? I wonder if you can do something for me. Can you get me some roles at your studio? I just want to come over to New Jersey and act for a few days a week so I can keep going to stage auditions. What do you think they'll pay me?"

"Well, I don't know," Estelle said.

"Will they give me fifteen dollars a day?"

Estelle paused as if she were thinking about it. "I think you might get a dollar or two a day if there is an opening, which I doubt there is."

"What? That's what they pay extras off the street. I've done *Shakespeare*, for God's sake."

"Dear friend, every fool has done Shakespeare."

In the harshest way possible, Estelle lectured

Annabel on everything she did not know about film acting, about the skill and experience of the actors, about camera angles, lighting, scenarios, and finally about how one must develop a name in films before one can earn the top money. As she was telling her all this, Estelle realized how much she actually had come to know about movie acting, how expert she was in the craft, and how it was a craft now, separate from stage acting. She hung up feeling a pride she had not felt before.

Henry handed out assignments for a pair of stories that required two days of location filming in New York City. One group was to go to a church on the East Side, the other to Jamaica Bay.
 "St. Joseph's has got a wrist bone of Saint Ann and thousands of people are showing up to be touched with it for its healing powers," he said. "In the bay, the naval reserves are having their war games. So a miracle healing story and a war story. I leave the details to you."
 Anxious to get everyone on the road, Henry took casting into his own hands, deciding that Bill, Margaret, and Jimmy would go off to do the healing story, and Estelle, Frank, and an agency actor (Marion had again called in sick) would go off to war.
 Using two studio autos, they took the ferry to Manhattan, then proceeded down Park Avenue,

competitively passing each other on the street. At one point, with Jimmy driving and the machine's canvas top pulled back, Margaret and Bill stood, put their arms around each other, and shimmied at Frank and Estelle in the other motor. It sent a chill through Estelle. She glanced over at Frank and observed his own misery at seeing his wife do that to him.

The automobiles parted company at 79th Street. The groups were to meet again that evening at a hotel in lower Manhattan and spend a second day filming before returning to New Jersey. However, the reserves' destroyers and submarines were not gathered in Jamaica Bay after all. The ships were all out in Gardiner's Bay on the end of Long Island, a hundred miles away. There were fishing trawlers and yachts in Jamaica Bay, though, so a story was quickly fashioned about a brother and sister, Frank and Estelle, orphaned by a fire and then adopted by different families, one rich, one poor. Twenty years pass and the sister's yacht is rammed by the brother's fishing boat, eventually leading to the dramatic reunion.

The scenes in the bay were shot by two o'clock. Then the three went in search of the Albert Hotel on the East Side.

Meanwhile, the other group had gone to the church and shot some film of the exterior, but because of the mobs of people, they could not get inside. ("You can't push by a line of sick people, saying 'Us first. We're picture people,'" Margaret would later tell Estelle.) So they went to the hotel at noon, had drinks in a bar next door, and then retired to their rooms – except that Bill and Margaret retired to the same room.

Reaching the hotel and being told the others were already there, Estelle got her room key and went upstairs. She found Frank in the hall, knocking repeatedly on the door of his and Margaret's room. A suffering look on his face, he was quietly pleading with Margaret to unlock it.

"What's she got, someone in there with her?" Estelle asked, intending a joke, but then she saw Frank's expression and realized the truth. Estelle reached over Frank and pounded on the door. In a deepened voice, she said, "Look here, I'm the manager's wife. What's going on? Open the door or I'll unlock it with my key."

The door opened in a moment and there were Bill and Margaret, clothed by this time, whether or not they had been so before. Their story was that they had gotten drunk and were too ashamed to open the door. There was, in fact, a gin bottle on a table. Margaret began to cry and Bill stood sheepishly off in the corner.

Estelle had seen Margaret cry when asked to on the set, and knew this was likely acting, yet Frank seemed to accept the story, telling Estelle in a whisper, "Margaret is vulnerable to liquor, and Bill says he stayed with her to make sure she didn't go out and drive somewhere."

Estelle had rented a house in Fort Lee to be closer to the studio, and several nights later Bill showed up, knocking on her window about two o'clock in the morning. He had driven back from a Trenton bar in the rain and thought he might have hit someone walking on the road. He had been drinking. His breath was the obvious evidence of that, and he wanted Estelle to drive him back out and see what they could find. ("You mean look for a body?" she asked. "Then what are we going to do if we find one?")

Estelle drove Bill's automobile, which did have a dent in the fender, but it was soon plain that he could not remember the route he had taken.

"Maybe you only hit a raccoon," she said.

They searched for nearly an hour, then parked on the side of a highway, somewhat lost, and Bill began to complain about what a miserable time he was having with Marion. He told Estelle how much he missed her and that he was thinking of leaving Marion. He wanted to stay with her that night, but Estelle would not let him.

The clouds broke and there was suddenly moonlight. A healthy spring aroma lifted off the rain-soaked dead leaves on the roadside, and wood frogs could be heard calling in nearby ponds. Bill begged Estelle to let him come home with her, crying a bit in his drunken despair. The auto's windows were open and she saw someone's dog, a shepherd, sitting opposite them on the road, just watching them in a dog's dignified way, hoping he would be called over to be petted. Estelle found herself admiring the dog, thinking how wonderful dogs could be. Then she glanced at Bill and heard his jabbering. She found at that moment that Bill and every man like him that she had ever met, men who once attracted her, whose bullying nature she mistook for strength, now disgusted her.

That was the effective end of Bill in her life. He had coffee in her kitchen to clear his head, but she still refused to let him stay, with no feelings within her that counseled her otherwise. At her demand to get out, he drove home to Marion.

A day later, though, Estelle heard that Marion had left Bill and quit Blanchard Brothers. She felt no guilt that the news pleased her.

13.

Second Avenue cafe

With the failure of Bill's marriage, it was not despondency he felt: it was relief. When he found Marion's letter saying she had gone home to her mother, he smoked a cigar on his back porch while his thoughts turned to women and the night life of New York.

In that city and elsewhere, the motion pictures were becoming respectable. In the Sunday newspapers, the profiles and photographs were as likely to be of actors and actresses in motion pictures as of those on stage. Nearly everywhere, the cheap movie houses were giving way to something better: grand buildings with splendid furnishings, rivaling any legitimate theatre.

With this rising status of movies and his established place in them ("The handsomest man in pictures" appeared on all his theatre posters), Bill felt he would now stand even with any man in his attractiveness to the city's beautiful women.

He waited two weeks to see if Marion would change her mind, and when he heard nothing from her, he put the furniture in storage, gave up the house, and sent half their savings, seven hundred dollars, to her through her mother. Then he rented an apartment near Central Park.

A bachelor stage actor who, like Bill, had risen from vaudeville, lived in the same building. On Bill's first night in the city, he went to a cafe on Second Avenue that the actor had recommended as a place to meet women. Within minutes of arriving, Bill's eyes fell on a woman unlike anyone he had ever seen before: beautiful green eyes, black hair, a fashionable black dress. She was unaccompanied, sipping a cocktail at the bar, conversing with a waiter.

"Exquisite," he would tell the actor the next day. "You know how New York is, though. You have all sorts of rich fellows in these places – sportsmen, even royalty. But she looks at me and it was clear she recognizes me. She must have seen my pictures. I could see I was someone to her. So instead of being a fellow in the crowd with no chance of this object of his desires having an interest in him, here I am the most likely. It was quite a moment, to want something this much and to be in a position to have it."

"So what happened?" the actor asked.

"Not much. She didn't speak English."

Bill and Margaret, with Jimmy Scanlon as the cameraman, were sent to nearby Ridgefield for scenes by a lake. The scenario had to do with a shipwreck and lovers stranded on an island. The kisses between Bill and Margaret became more passionate than intended, and late in the day, after dropping Jimmy at the studio, Bill and Margaret took their ardor to its conclusion in a hotel on the west side of Manhattan.

Hurried and nervous, they found not only that the physical act was artless and unsatisfying but that the conversation in bed afterward was eerily that of an unhappily married couple. Bill smoked. Margaret drank seltzer and gin. There was no humor to any of what they said. It was as if they were passing time in the company's Ford during a rain delay on location. They gossiped jealously about other actors, grumbled about money, and gossiped some more. Margaret complained at length about Frank's stinginess with their money and his "dour nature."

"He never does anything just for fun. There always has to be a purpose."

"So why did you marry him?" Bill asked.

"Because that's who you marry: Frank and Marion and people like that – dependable people. Not people like us. I wouldn't marry someone like us. Look, despite what I may say about him, Frank always makes sure the bills get paid, he never forgets my birthday, he won't let me do all the things I know I oughtn't, and he listens to me even when *I* wouldn't listen to me."

"Those aren't reasons. You don't love him."

"Well, I don't *not* love him, if you know what I mean, so I love him."

"What do you mean, people like us?"

"Like us, like we know we are. You know how you are."

"No, I don't."

"Well, don't make me tell you."

After a silence, Margaret began to cry softly. Bill did not ask why, instead getting up to wash. As she lay alone in bed, Margaret's crying gave way to a long confession of her marriage sins and why she now regretted each one of them.

"Frank is dependable. That's exactly what he is. It's the best thing of all that a man can be. God, oh, God!"

Bill dressed and went down to the hotel's bar. He did not see Margaret leave, but as he settled the bill about midnight, the desk man said she had.

On the street, Bill argued with a police officer over his illegally parked motor and was arrested for drunkenness. He woke up the next morning in a jail cell, surrounded by vagrants and petty criminals. As a result, he was infested with body lice and had to submit to a chemical bath administered by his dentist to get rid of them.

Reading the *Bergen County Tribune*, Bill saw a letter about a pedestrian death in Trenton some weeks earlier, caused by a Ford. Even though the car he had been driving the night he hit something on the road was a Buick, his heart began to race.

> Is it not evident that the automobile is becoming a slayer as much as a conveyor of people? In the annual report of the Highways Protective Society, it is noted that automobiles are rivaling the horse and wagon as a killer of people walking on the streets of New York City. In 1911 the tally stood at 142 fatalities for motors and 172 for wagons. In not another few years, we all know the balance will slip to automobiles and motor trucks. It is inevitable. In Trenton just a few weeks ago, a woman was run down by a Ford sedan without the driver even showing her the mercy to stop. Had she been taken to a hospital, she might have survived. As it is, she died

and the operator of that vehicle now must live with his guilt until his own judgment day arrives.

Bill telephoned the Trenton station house.

"This is Sergeant Foley."

"Yes," Bill said. "I'd like to inquire about the woman killed a few weeks ago by an automobile. The *Tribune* mentioned it today. Can you give me any details?"

"Why do you want to know?" The voice was gruff and suspicious.

"I read about it in the paper and thought there might be a place to donate to the family."

"What they didn't say is the woman had been drinking. She was a prostitute we knew very well."

"Oh, was she?"

"She's got a sister who's in the same line, so don't donate any money to anyone. You'd just be supporting their evil profession. Keep your money, my friend. Keep your pity, too, is what I say."

14.

Theatre broadside

Unable to go on location just before Christmas because of snow, Frank and Estelle devised a small film, *Aunt Jane*, about a maiden aunt, played by Estelle, who issued sage advice to her troublesome niece, played by a per diem actress. The inexpensive drama, done entirely on the studio set, was hugely popular. Henry, enthusiastic about the profits, suggested it be turned into their first series. They quickly did seven installments, releasing a new one weekly through the winter. They made Estelle a leading name in film, giving the studio its first cover story in *Photoplay* in February of 1912.

The *New York Times*, in criticizing the city's controller, said, "If only our politicians could have the common sense of the moving pictures' Aunt Jane. Think of the efficiency. Think of the savings."

Henry, normally aloof toward the actors, began to treat Estelle differently from the others, sometimes calling her into his office to chat. He would confide in her, telling her details of the studio's finances or of Charles' continuing troubles with alcohol. Discharged from the sanitarium, he had relapsed and been readmitted. The attention surprised and gratified Estelle. When Frank and Margaret resigned from the company in March (Margaret was unexpectedly pregnant and Frank wanted to return home to the South), her place at the studio only became more prominent.

One day, Estelle received a call from Mrs. Douglas Robinson, the sister of former president Theodore Roosevelt. The colonel was coming to New York City to deliver campaign speeches on the East Side in support of candidates on the eve of the Republican National Convention.

Would Estelle like to join a group of Republican women for dinner and the rounds of assembly rooms and meeting halls? "However, I'm embarrassed to say I don't know your name except as Aunt Jane."

"Well, I don't know *your* name except by your husband's or brother's name."

The woman laughed. "It's Corinne."

"It's Estelle."

The dinner at the Waldorf-Astoria featured Foster salad and brook trout with sauce au bleu. The conversation was eclectic: the Nobel for Madame Curie, the turkey trot, the theft of the *Mona Lisa* in Paris, Nijinsky, the new chef at the Hotel Knickerbocker, and, of course, the tragedy of the *Titanic*. Everyone at the table, except Estelle, seemed to know someone rich or famous or both who had gone down with the liner. Still, Estelle felt an unanticipated ease in the company of these women. *How odd*, she thought. They were all important, heads of social agencies or wives of well-known politicians, yet she, a mere actress, was an equal in their eyes.

Later, they joined Roosevelt as he stumped at the New Star Casino on 107th Street. The women sat on the platform as the feisty politician spoke. However, in the center of the crowded hall, a tiny woman stood on her chair and shouted, "How about votes for women, Colonel?"

Others in the hall shouted, "Put her out!" However, Roosevelt tried to answer her, saying he favored a referendum for women to express their opinion on the suffrage.

"That's no answer!" the woman shouted, still up on her chair, and the hall again erupted in boos and demands for the woman's eviction.

Two of the ladies beside Estelle booed as well, which surprised her. Eventually, the suffragette was dragged out by ushers, to the cheers of some on the platform.

Afterward, the women returned to Mrs.

Robinson's home in Manhattan, and the evening was assessed over tea, with much of the discussion centered on the new breed of militant suffrage fighters. Hearing mean criticism from some, Estelle stayed quiet.

The women's vote, in her opinion, was the preeminent issue of the era. In her early days in road companies, in her spare time she had read history books bought in antiquarian shops. The lesson that emerged was that civilization marched forward but most people did not. The average man or woman often opposed progress, even when the benefit and moral rightness of it were evident. It was her opinion that only tumultuous events, wars or civil uprisings, would make progress stick. So she saw the suffragettes, no matter their tactics, as necessary and good. That there were women who were cautious about suffrage astounded her, though. Yet some of these distinguished women around her were.

One who had attained a law degree before having her family told Estelle she actually opposed gaining the vote. "I'm no critic of my sex's merits. On the contrary, I see the great things that we're doing around the country, bettering industrial conditions and establishing traveling libraries. However, we don't allow our men to vote until they've reached twenty-one, yet they train for their responsibility from birth. Can we allow women to vote who have no training? If we did, it would be to the peril of society."

Estelle was astonished. She knew that this woman would stay in her thoughts as the example of what not to become in her own life.

15.

Longstreet's kitchen

As Bill's contract was about to run out, Henry called him in to renegotiate, though both knew it was futile, that Bill had no intention of staying. Henry suggested a figure of one hundred and forty dollars a week. Bill did not even respond. He walked out of the office and Henry passed the word to everyone not to give him any leading roles during his final two weeks. On his last Friday, Bill gathered his personal supplies, and without saying a word to Henry, he left at noon, slipping out the back door.

However, Bill already had a job in place with an independent studio in Brooklyn: Champion Films, which specialized in Westerns made on a dairy farm on Long Island. The studio had never used known actors before. Although offered a yearlong contract at one hundred and fifty dollars a week, Bill asked instead to be hired day to day at a lesser figure, believing that in six months he would be worth many times as much. The films he did for Champion fared no better than those with unknowns, though, and by the fall he found there were few days he got calls from the studio.

However, Bill lent his name and face to a series of magazine advertisements for Huyler's Chocolates and Sterling Castle cigars that fattened his bank account considerably. Although he was able to get per diem work that winter with Thanhouser in New Rochelle, perhaps a day or two a week, he grew idle and indolent. He got in the habit of pouring a drink the moment he woke up, and spent many days in saloons in his neighborhood. Self-made rich men who desired to be around actors paid for the drinks and taxis.

He met a man in a bar one afternoon, Arthur Longstreet, a financier, who said he was interested in learning about the monetary side of the motion-picture business. Would Bill educate him over dinner? Longstreet had his chauffeur bring his motor around, a Rolls-Royce Silver Ghost. His apartment was on Park Avenue. In fact, he had bought two apartments in the cooperative building and had the walls between them broken down for more space. The floors were cedar, and oil paintings hung on every wall. In the largest room, which fronted the avenue, there was a grand piano and a combination pipe and reed organ, operated by electricity.

"Before the Spanish war, it was easy to get servants, mainly German and English girls, but they feared New York being bombed and went home. Now it's difficult to find anyone capable," Longstreet said.

He showed Bill the kitchen, which was fit for a restaurant. He introduced his personal chef, an Austrian who spoke little English but smiled continually. Longstreet boasted of being able to get green corn in January and strawberries year-round, of having sturgeon brought in live from Russia and asparagus shipped from Argentina. In the wine room, he showed Bill bottles of 1831 Chateau Lafitte, bought for him in Paris at an auction when Restaurant Durand cleaned out its cellars.

The meal was lamb cutlets served with green peas. The dessert was iced peaches in essence of violets.

"So let me ask you," Longstreet said, "what's it like being such a toast of the picture world?"

He questioned Bill about the finances of moviemaking, asking him what part of the profits an actor would earn on a picture. Bill told him that most actors make very little. Longstreet asked him how he felt about that, "given that you're the reason people pay their money to see these pictures?"

Bill, feeling the accumulation of the day's alcohol, mumbled something about injustice. Longstreet took hold of Bill's arm, leaning in as if about to say something important.

"Look. What I really want is to back a film company, and you may be just the fellow to run it. What advice would you give me about making motion pictures?"

Bill recovered his wits with coffee and talked enthusiastically for a good hour about the plots that worked, whom to hire, whom to stay away from, sets, cameras, advertising: all the things that he had absorbed in just two years making movies. Longstreet took it in, to Bill's eyes, with rapt attention, as if what Bill was saying were the words of a prophet.

Soon they were making drawings on linen napkins: studio layouts, set locations, directions of morning and afternoon sun, offices. Eventually, they wrote down the elements of a contract. Longstreet would buy the building in which the studio could be constructed, paying for all the needed renovations. Bill would purchase cameras, film, lighting, and other equipment.

In the end, Longstreet would own the physical studio and all equipment, and Bill would own all the films, giving Longstreet half the profits to each for the first two years of its issue. From Bill's standpoint, it all favored Bill.

The evening ended with cigars, brandy, and the Metropolitan Opera on the phonograph. Bill was certain he had never had a moment of such bliss and satisfaction. He vowed to own a residence as fine as Longstreet's within a year. He was certain he would.

The next day, feeling no less confident about the deal, Bill set about looking for an available warehouse in the city. However, that night the telephone rang and it was Marion. Her voice, familiar as it was, startled him, like a voice in a graveyard. She said she had received some overdue bills of his, which had been forwarded to her, so she paid them. She was now living on her cousin's farm in Connecticut. Bill promised to pay her back immediately, saying he would mail her a bank draft. That settled, they talked at first in a reserved manner, like new acquaintances getting to know each other.

"Are you enjoying acting these days?" Marion asked.

"I enjoy it, yes. I feel I'm better suited for it now than I was."

"I thought you were naturally good when you first began."

"Thank you for the compliment."

Then, abruptly, Marion asked him what he intended for their marriage. "Do you think you want it to resume?"

"I don't . . . I haven't . . . I haven't been thinking about it, because I didn't think there was anything to think about. You left. You walked out."

There was silence. Without thinking, only intending to give himself time, he said it would be better if they talked about "such important matters later when we can take some time to be thorough about it. This isn't a good time for me."

"Why don't we meet, then?" Marion said. "Why don't I take a train down to New York?"

Flustered, he agreed. Though he did not mean it as a hopeful sign, he realized that she would take it as such. They set a time and place, but after hanging up he decided that he had made a mistake. When they were first married, he knew that Marion felt his career was competition for his attentions. She liked nothing better than to spend the day sitting on the sofa, listening to the Victrola or reading the newspaper, snuggling. If he took his arm from around her, she would grab it back. If he was late returning from a location, she would act as if he were personally responsible. He knew his running a movie company would only make the distractions for him worse than before. He could already hear her voice in the corner of his thoughts, chiding him, complaining, sulking.

At the same time, he believed he was ready for marriage now. These months of bachelorhood, of women coming in and out of his life, had made him desire the constancy of marriage. He thought he might be good at it this time around.

On the day they were to meet, he spent the morning looking at two warehouses in the Bronx with Longstreet and did not monitor his pocket watch. Arriving at the restaurant nearly fifteen minutes late, he found Marion sitting by herself near the window.

The first thing she said was that his lateness had caused her to be "an object of pity for the passing crowds."

Bill thought, "Well, here it's already starting."

He took a seat, they were handed menus, and in the long silence as they studied the offerings, he gathered his manners, attempting to start again. They talked politely about her train trip into the city, the changes in New York in just a year, the construction, the automobiles jamming the streets, and the noticeable disappearance of horses. Then, asked what he was doing lately, Bill mentioned the deal he had struck with Longstreet.

A frown immediately appeared on Marion's face, slowly turning to disappointment as Bill explained the details.

"So what do you think?" he asked.

She seemed to be weighing what to say as she took a sip of water. "Honestly, I think running a movie business is for the bankers and those people, the smart people, not the people like you and me, Bill."

He stared at her as anger rose in him. "What do you mean, like you and me? You think I'm stupid, don't you?"

"I don't. It's just that we're . . . you and I . . . we're not educated."

"You mean we're not the kind of people to do any more than have a little house and grow tomatoes in the garden and remark at the weather all day long."

"No, that's not what I mean."

"The problem is, you look at acting as nothing really, just this strange occupation where simpletons can make a lot of money and get a lot of attention for doing nothing at all. That may be you, but it's not me."

With that eruption of temper, Bill knew that nothing between them had changed and that any chance their marriage could be mended had disappeared. He stared at the menu in silence. Then, without looking again at Marion, he dropped money on the table and left.

16.

The matinee

After walking out on her marriage, Marion initially had gone home to her mother but was told to "go back to your own home, to your husband, and beg his forgiveness on your knees."

Instead, she went to stay with her cousin on her farm in Enfield, Connecticut. She milked cows, fed hogs, plucked chickens, fashioned candles from beeswax, and beat clothes to cleanliness in a washtub until her fingertips were raw. She had hoped the simplicity of physical labor would mend her spirit, but it only tired her body, doing nothing for her soul. Making matters worse, she felt growing resentment from her cousin, a stout girl whose husband turned and gazed at Marion unashamedly whenever she entered the room and who sometimes stood outside her bedroom door in the middle of the night, breathing irregularly.

She had gone down to New York to meet Bill, knowing that her life was at a desperate point. However, in retrospect, the hour and thirty-six minutes between stepping off the train from Connecticut in Grand Central Station to reboarding the train on the same station platform did not seem to exist. Just as dreams are fiercely real in the mind as they are experienced but fade into a fog on waking, so Marion could not reconstruct anything of the lunch. She could not recall what Bill wore, what their greeting had been, or what the details of the argument were that followed. The only lasting image for her was of Bill angrily leaving the table.

Knowing she could not stay on her cousin's farm but still estranged from her mother, Marion rented a room in Hartford and found employment in the city's public library. However, shelving books was no more consolation to her than farm work, and soon she had the added worry that such jobs were all she would ever be suited for, given that she had failed to graduate from high school.

On her application for the library position, she had written "moving picture actress" under previous work experience, believing in the value of truthfulness. Soon everyone in the library, clerks and patrons alike, knew of her background, but instead of admiration, it aroused whispers and rumors. What had happened that she had fallen so far? Her one friend among the clerks told her the leading theory was that she had disgraced herself with a child out of wedlock. Marion denied this but declined to tell the woman of her failed marriage, thinking it would be held nearly as disgraceful.

She began to contemplate a return to films. While she knew Blanchard Brothers would not take her back, there were other studios around New York City. Then she read an article in the *Hartford Courant* about the decline of the movie industry in the East and the move to the West Coast by many film companies. It also spoke of the wave of well-known stage actors and actresses jumping to motion pictures. A sharp fear ran through her. Had her name been forgotten? Would other studios even consider her now? Films were quickly moving on to features of two reels, even four reels. Serials were the rage. Her time was surely passing.

She wrote to the Thanhouser Studio in New Rochelle, north of New York City, asking if they might use her. She detailed her films, giving a dozen titles and her role in each. The head of the studio wrote her back a polite letter, saying that unfortunately he had only recently come to New York from Chicago and did not recognize her name, confirming Marion's fears. However, he offered her extra work at two dollars a day "should you be the type of actress that is pleasing to the camera and should we have need of any but our regular players on a particular day." With no actual promise of a job, and after investigating the circuitous path of trains and trolleys to reach New Rochelle, she did not pursue it.

A custodian at the library told her that a local movie house was showing one of her Blanchard Brothers pictures, *The Free Spirit,* apparently to fill out a short bill. Marion went to the matinee. A Jack London story, *The Sea Wolf,* was the lead film. Hers was shown after a newsreel of China.

She played a young girl who danced in a city park in a summer rainstorm, twirling on the lawn, a picture of unrestrained joy as the shower drenched her. She caught the eye of a policeman on the beat, played by Bill, but as he crossed the park to introduce himself, she ran off. Smitten, the policeman searched for her for days, finally discovering her in a dress shop, waiting on customers. The film ended with the title, "It is the promise of love and not rain that is in the air now." Estelle and Margaret played customers and Frank played the shop owner. It was made in June of 1911, just after the company went up to West Haverstraw.

In the darkened theatre now, with cigar smoke drifting through the projected light, Marion watched the dancing girl as if it were someone else on screen and not herself. She almost wanted to cry, feeling she had little connection left to the world of motion pictures, as if she were a dead spirit in the afterworld, allowed one last look at the life she left behind. She envied that girl, more as actress than as character, envied her freedom, her opportunities, but she wished with all her heart that she could warn her about the things that were about to happen in her life.

When Bill appeared on screen, her breath nearly left her. A door flew fully open onto this world she had almost forgotten. Then, in the shop scenes, when she saw Estelle and Margaret, she could not contain her emotions any longer. She cried softly in the dark, as much at a larger recognition as at seeing them all. Her world then, her world now – the contrast was overwhelming. For the first time, she truly understood the mistake that leaving Blanchard Brothers had been, a mistake that might never be undone.

17.

The patents' men

Bill found a vacant warehouse in Brooklyn, which Longstreet inspected and approved. The two sketched out renovations over lunch. Within a week, loads of lumber and plumbing supplies were delivered to the site. Cameras and lights were purchased and film and developing chemicals were ordered. Bill contacted a Biograph scenarist and bought two stories. In one, a circus troupe's acrobat saves people caught in an apartment fire. In the other, a sea captain collapses at the helm, so his wife takes over the ship, navigating through storm-tossed seas to deliver the cargo on time.

As construction of the set was completed, three tough-looking men visited the studio. They said they represented the Motion Picture Patents Company and demanded to see Bill's camera.

("We need to know if it's in violation.")

Bill lied, saying the camera had not been delivered yet. In fact, it was in the trunk of his Buick. The men said they would be back in a few days. Bill had heard of the patents trust, but he had not expected it to bother him. He had been told that Thomas Edison and a few other studio owners put it together. They had all the patents and were trying to keep out the independents, requiring them to pay a steep fee to use any of the patented equipment. Bills's camera was one of the patented models.

When he had been acting for Blanchard Brothers, Bill once heard Charles boast that they were using a patented camera and paid nothing for the privilege. Yet no patents men ever seemed to bother them. Why would they bother an even smaller outfit like his? He called Jimmy Scanlon, who had an explanation.

"The Blanchards' father was a friend of Edison, so they had permission or some kind of license, I guarantee you. But I heard about directors for other independents getting beat up for using patent cameras. I'd be careful if I were you."

Bill telephoned the trust's office in Philadelphia. He said he was a stage director from Boston who was thinking of turning one of his plays into a movie.

"I'm inquiring what a license would cost to make films."

"I'm not sure. I'm not the regular secretary. But I would imagine it would be in the hundreds of dollars."

"Per year?"

"No. Per film."

Bill hung up in a panic. His contract with Longstreet said he was responsible for the cost of all licenses and permits. By the next day, though, he had devised a plan. He bought a second camera, a Swiss model that worked poorly but infringed on no trust patent. He would always have that on the set, but he would use the patent camera when it came time to film. He also hired two bodyguards and bought a Smith and Wesson revolver.

On the day they began shooting the circus story, he assembled the actors and warned them of the potential trouble. ("These sons of bitches are nothing but criminals. We may have to make a fight of it to get these movies done.") At the mention of possible gunplay, two actors quit on the spot.

Bill kept his revolver atop the camera. He filmed the story about the acrobats and the fire first. Behind the brick warehouse, a fire was set with scrap wood and gasoline beneath a second-story window. Beyond the fire a net was positioned. A trapeze artist, hired for the day from Barnum and Bailey, somersaulted out the window, over the fire and into the net with a bundle in his arms, meant to be a baby. He dived out a second time with a store dummy of a man on his back, then a third time with a dummy of a woman. Other stunts were improvised and executed. The crew cheered excitedly, sure that an excellent film was going to be the result.

Just before dawn the next morning, Bill pulled up to the warehouse and saw lights on inside. Unfortunately, his revolver was also inside. He crept to a window and saw two men in the shadows going through boxes and cabinets. Bill waited until they went into the office, then he sneaked inside to find his tool chest, which contained the Smith and Wesson.

Before he reached it, he was interrupted by one of the men who leveled his own revolver at Bill. "We want to see your camera."

"You want to see it? It's in there." Bill pointed to a small trunk nearby.

The man with the revolver put it in his belt momentarily and bent down to open the trunk lid. At the same time, Bill opened his tool chest, intending to grab his revolver. The other man pulled out a knife.

"What are you reaching for?"

"I think maybe the camera is actually in here. Let me see." Bill reached in, snatched the revolver, and shot a round past the men, who fled through the door, dragging the small trunk with them. Only then did Bill remember that the trunk they grabbed contained his last four reels of undeveloped film, and it was Eastman film under one of the trust's patents.

The men returned that afternoon, but this time with a lawyer who demanded again to see Bill's camera. With his own bodyguards at his side, wearing their own revolvers, Bill was ready. He showed them the Swiss camera. The six of them stood in a circle, trading mean stares and strong words.

The lawyer brought up the issue of the patented film and demanded license payments "or else there will be trouble." Bill agreed to pay twenty dollars to get his reels back.

However, he arrived at the warehouse the next morning to find some negatives scissored up, including the footage of the first day's fire stunts, and no one on the premises to blame.

After rehiring the acrobat and repeating the stunts, Bill completed *The Rose Street Fire*, a two-reeler. He began making plans for the second film, the sea picture, which he ambitiously considered making in four reels using elaborate sets. He also began selling the first film, visiting exchanges and theatres.

He learned a hard fact, though. No one was buying films directly from independents anymore. Exhibitors leased blocks of films from the large studios through the exchanges, getting discounts for them, so there was no room on the bill for other single purchases. It was all-or-nothing buying.

"It's absolutely closed up," Bill told Longstreet

over lunch. "The industry changed and no one told us."

Bill noticed Longstreet's seeming indifference.

"So what do you think you'll do?" Longstreet asked. He bit into his roast beef sandwich, taking the news as if he had no part in the studio.

"What will I do? Well, I don't know," Bill said, still trying to absorb Longstreet's unworried reaction.

Bill drove up to Westchester to see a friend who ran an exchange. He owned a farm in White Plains and controlled the film territory for Westchester County. Theatre owners would come to him to rent films. Bill offered to knock down the price of his film if he would offer it through the exchange. The friend had a projector in his barn, so a bed sheet was thrown over a rafter, and Bill, the friend, and the friend's two young daughters sat on overturned buckets as the film ran.

The friend said to his daughters, "Now, look at this picture and tell me what you think." Then he said to Bill, "They're the public, the public reaction. You and I, because we're in the business, we don't see things like the public. So it's their opinion what counts."

As the film began, the Holstein cows in the stalls shifted about, mooing and occasionally dropping patties in the hay. The girls barely paid attention, complaining continually about the uncomfortable buckets. Even when the circus acrobat performed on the trapeze, they seemed bored, commenting that he was not as good as those in a circus they went to at the Hippodrome.

Asked by their father what they thought about the film when it ended, both girls just shrugged.

"I like elephants," one daughter said. "Is there going to be any elephants in this? They're from Africa."

"I could add elephants," Bill said.

"I like tigers, not elephants," the other daughter said.

When Bill did not offer to add tigers also, there was an awkward silence. Nevertheless, as a favor to Bill, the friend said he would use his film as a filler title, making it clear that if it did not prove to be popular, "then I have to drop it."

18.

The suffragettes march

Emmeline Pankhurst, the militant English suffragette, was traveling to New York aboard the steamship *Provence* in October of 1913 to speak in the city. Estelle asked Henry Blanchard for permission to make a scenario around the event, with herself playing a woman like Mrs. Pankhurst.

Although personally ambivalent about the women's vote, Henry decided there could be profit in such a film. In America, as in England, the interest in suffrage was at a high pitch. A phrase was increasingly heard: "lawless women." Suffragettes recently marched in Newark, packing rocks in their aprons to throw at police officers. In London, they wielded hammers and smashed windows.

Blanchard Brothers, by Henry's admission, was

in its waning days. Of the original group, only Estelle and Jimmy Scanlon remained. Estelle now wrote, directed, and starred in any films Blanchard Brothers issued, perhaps four or five a month, using agency actors and actresses to fill other roles.

Henry told her he was trying to find a buyer for the studio, feeling that the name still counted for something in the industry. However, it was Estelle's view that his reluctance to move to longer feature films – he would allow her only two reels per film – had dimmed the studio's early reputation for excellence, which had been forged in West Haverstraw.

Estelle had grown active in the suffrage movement. In March of 1913, she went to Washington to be part of a suffrage parade down Pennsylvania Avenue preceding President Wilson's inauguration. More than five thousand women took part, carrying the placards of their states, wearing the yellow ribbons emblematic of their movement. The police were inadequate to control the hundreds of thousands of spectators along the route. In places, the crowds pushed into the procession of women, and men jeered and insulted the suffragettes. (A mounted police officer yelled at Estelle, "If my wife were where you are, I would break open her head.") The experience only fortified her resolve to do whatever she could for the cause.

The *Provence* and Mrs. Pankhurst were set to

clear quarantine in New York Harbor at seven o'clock in the morning, so Estelle and Jimmy Scanlon prepared to board the ship along with a cadre of reporters and photographers, expecting to accompany Mrs. Pankhurst into the city. However, at the pier they learned that a hearing was to be convened in the music room on the promenade deck of the liner to determine if causes existed – namely moral turpitude – to bar Mrs. Pankhurst from entering the United States. The immigration inspectors assembled, and Mrs. Pankhurst arrived in a sealskin coat with a blue cloth hat topped by a plume. She was accompanied by her entourage of international suffragettes. Estelle thought her appearance magnificent.

The interrogation was brief: "Have you been convicted of arson?"

"I have not. My last conviction was for conspiracy."

She was told she would have to be taken to Ellis Island to appear before a Board of Special Inquiry. Then Mrs. Pankhurst proceeded outside to the deck, to give interviews to reporters. When Estelle introduced herself, Mrs. Pankhurst said she recognized her from her films, which she said played widely in England. They spoke of the importance motion pictures could have in presenting the social philosophy behind the suffrage effort. Estelle saw a sparkle in Mrs. Pankhurst's eyes, a delight almost, at the melodrama unfolding around her.

Standing nearby on the deck, the band of the *Provence* played ragtime. "Oh, Those Pretty Blue Eyes." The two women stopped to listen. Estelle thought it wonderful: the music, the sea air. She felt the exhilaration at that moment of being at the center of history, of feeling the muscled push of progress all around her.

Mrs. Pankhurst attended the hearing on Ellis Island, and within an hour she was ordered deported, her time in the interim to be spent confined to rooms on the island. The counsel for Mrs. Pankhurst said the finding would be appealed to Washington.

Two days later, President Wilson would order her released and admitted to the country. However, immediately after the hearing, speaking to reporters, Mrs. Pankhurst, who was famous for her hunger strikes in Holloway Prison in London, threatened such a strike during her incarceration on the island. With this, Estelle could feel her pulse race. She thought of her film and of the great drama to be portrayed.

Returning to Fort Lee before noon, she had Jimmy prepare the set and call an agency for actors. Estelle telephoned Henry at his home, excitedly relating to him the turn of events, saying she was rewriting the scenario to reflect them. Henry interrupted her, saying he must see the story before anyone was hired or any filming began. Estelle paused, then asked why.

"Why? Well, I was speaking to men at my club about this. They had some concerns, which I think I have as concerns, too. I'll come in to the studio."

For the half hour before he arrived, Estelle rewrote the scenario using all the dramatic talents she had acquired. The story revolved around an English woman whose husband's tyranny in their home leads her to become a suffragette. In her travels abroad for the movement, she finds respect that she never had in her own house.

When she heard Henry come in the studio's rear door, she met him by his office. They spoke of the fine weather as he hung his coat, both deliberately avoiding the pages in her hand.

"Well, let's see what we have," he finally said.

Estelle sat opposite his desk as he read the scenario. He took an especially long time, she thought. He used a pencil to cross out sections and to make notes in others, his expression gradually turning sour. Estelle felt the approach of a difficult moment. Confrontation was in the air, she feared. She cautioned herself not to say regrettable things.

"Look," Henry said, "I want to see other sides of this question in the story. There must be a character, a kindly figure, say a senator or someone, who will speak some wisdom to this woman. She advocates hooligan tactics. He should be the voice of experience. He must tell her the vote will come to women but at the right time. To hurry it would only . . . What is this? 'Give us the vote or give us death.' Do these women actually say that?"

"Many do."

"What fools."

Estelle had to strain to keep quiet.

"Look here," Henry said. "Something else I want is this. We all know that many men living in tenements are not capable of voting intelligently. That's widely acknowledged although few are willing to say it. But I think someone should say it in this story. The point should be made that how can we give the vote to their women in the tenements who, on the average, are even less capable than the men? Do you see?"

Estelle stared at Henry. His undisguised contempt for the poor, of whose class Estelle had been in her life, was suddenly too much. She stood at her chair now.

"I won't change this scenario. If you order it, I'll quit," she said.

Henry looked up with a start. He appeared about to answer such an overbearing challenge in his usual manner, but he paused, aware of the larger moment that had been created. He closed his eyes and rubbed them with a single finger on each hand, as if visited by a migraine. Then, in a quiet voice that seemed to have no anger in it, but rather humility and compassion, he said he had decided to shutter the doors of the studio.

"I've wanted to go home to Michigan for a while. This seems the right time. However, thank you, Estelle, for what you've done for Blanchard Brothers. Thank you deeply."

He then got up from the desk, came around, and silently embraced her in a lingering hug. A bit stunned, Estelle was not immediately sure if she was to finish the film or not. She waited in Henry's outer office until she heard him on the back lot telling Jimmy to disassemble the set and store the furniture and props in the barn. With that, she collected her belongings and went home, not turning to take a final look at the studio until she was well down Linwood Avenue.

19.

The Tombs

It had been their agreement that Longstreet would have no hand in the filmmaking, that he was strictly Bill's uninvolved partner. However, he began to visit the studio in the afternoons, at first standing well behind the camera, observing silently. When film was being edited, though, or scenarios worked out, he started to offer suggestions, something Bill at first politely accommodated but then began to resent. He tried to think of a way to discourage Longstreet, short of insulting him, but he had waited too long. Longstreet had already insinuated himself into the process.

While Bill made plans for the second story he had bought, the sea story, he contacted a booking agency to send him an actress for another story, which he had written himself, about a rich woman falling in love with a carpenter, whom Bill planned to play. ("I'm looking for a society type. In fact, try to find a society woman. They have their own wardrobe and jewelry. Maybe a former actress who married rich.")

Alice Fairchild, the wife of a Sutton Place surgeon, arrived the next morning at the Brooklyn studio in a Pierce Arrow with a chauffeur. She was blonde with exquisitely large eyes. Bill had changed his mind, though, figuring that a wealthy woman would not lower herself to produce the histrionics that were required on the screen to affect an audience. However, in the absence of any other candidates, he decided to rehearse some scenes with her, taking notice, as she removed her coat, of the shapely figure beneath.

He explained the role to her. "You're a countess and you have to put it over that you're attracted to this nice young fellow, but at the same time you hold back because you're a good married woman, even though it's a bad marriage. It takes a great talent to convey all that without speaking. You have to act as if your body below the neck desires this carpenter one hundred percent, but your eyes are acting a hundred percent as if you know you oughtn't."

In the scene, the carpenter repairs a porch while the countess stands behind him, struggling with her emotions. Bill placed a chair where the carpenter was supposed to be, and had her act to it. The two set builders, the two bodyguards, the cameraman, the accountant, the chauffeur, and a guard dog looked on. Alice turned to Bill for the signal to begin. He nodded and she stepped to the chair. Taking a deep breath, she bit her lip and pounded her fist against her temple as if wracked with a powerful ambivalence. When she finished, Bill applauded enthusiastically, prompting others to do the same.

They did the scene again, this time with film, lighting, costumes, and Bill in place of the chair. In the afternoon, they moved about a mile away to a dead-end street. In the story, the countess receives a call that an accident has occurred on the road and that her husband might be a victim, so she rushes out to the scene. Of course, if it is true, it means she does not have to restrain her emotions for the carpenter any longer.

Once they began filming at the location, the police detective, played by one of Bill's bodyguards, showed Alice the dead man, played by the other bodyguard, as he lay on the roadside. Improvising, Alice fell to her knees and caressed the cheek of her husband. When she stood up, one of her knees was bleeding, but she maintained her character, something Bill saw as the mark of a professional.

The next day, Bill allowed Longstreet to look at the footage.

"I think she's great," Bill said.

"To be honest, I don't know. She seems . . .

cold, like she's not trying very hard."

Bill restrained his growing contempt for Longstreet. "I think a lot comes over. You feel every emotion she feels."

"I think you're starting to make bad business decisions," Longstreet said.

Bill did not even acknowledge the comment. When the street scene appeared, Longstreet observed that in black and white the blood on Alice's leg looked like mud.

"I thought you were going to make the story about a husband that cheats on the countess and that's why she chooses the carpenter. That's the better story."

"This story's fine. The husband dies," Bill said.

"I like the cheating story. Let's change it back."

In Longstreet's voice, Bill suddenly heard Henry Blanchard, the same insipid, meddling tone. Minutes later, they got into an argument about hair color. Longstreet wanted Alice to dye her hair black. He said blonde was cheap. Bill said heroines did not have dark hair.

"Think about it. Mary Pickford doesn't have black hair. She has golden locks. Mignon Anderson. Golden hair. Any of your heroines, the stars who audiences pay to see, they've got light-colored hair. The vamps and the villains are all dark-haired."

Longstreet, as if intending to finally and fully assert himself, demanded she dye her hair at least brown. Bill turned to Longstreet and defiantly refused. At that, they grew silent, both apparently wondering who would emerge from the argument with what he wanted.

In succeeding days, Longstreet stopped appearing at the studio in the afternoon. However, when Bill talked to him on the telephone, there seemed to be no hard feelings. Perhaps Longstreet saw it in his self-interest financially to leave him alone, Bill thought. He lied and told Longstreet he was receiving good reports from his exchange friend in Westchester, that the circus picture was getting returning patrons and that more theatres were booking it. In fact, only two theatres had booked it in a week.

Bill decided that of all his stories only the sea story had the range of great emotions and action that would fully capture the public's attention. He and Alice, who was to play the wife of the stricken sea captain, spent more and more time together, talking about costumes and shooting angles and approaches to the characters.

Meanwhile, Longstreet was able to convince a principal theatre in Chicago to run *The Countess and the Carpenter,* which Bill had completed, as a personal favor, and two newspapers there agreed to review it. Longstreet told Bill he considered the showing a test. As it turned out, the newspapers were critical of the movie and especially of Alice. The reviewer at the *Chicago Daily News* called the movie "an old story told in the same old way" and referred to Alice as "Miss I-can't-smile-or-cry-because-it-will-bring-wrinkles."

Bill and Longstreet stopped meeting for lunch and rarely talked on the telephone. At the studio, Bill grew morose, spending long hours alone in his office with Alice, writing and rewriting the sea scenario but also talking more personally with her. She confided that she was considering leaving her husband. ("When I'm here in the studio, I feel like a full woman. At home, my husband has less respect for me than for his hospital nurses.")

They dismissed her driver one afternoon and drove her motor out to Glen Cove on Long Island, parking by a deserted stretch of beach. Amid the tall sea grass and cold ocean breezes in the dunes, they submitted to their passion. Bill felt a healthiness to the act that he had not felt in years.

Two days later, Alice told Bill she had consulted with an attorney about filing a suit of divorce. Bill hastily wrote Marion in Connecticut, getting her address through her cousin in Enfield. He also asked for a divorce. He said he would pay for all the legal matters.

Marion's letter of reply was curt and emotionless. "Do whatever you feel is necessary. I will not make an argument against it."

Meanwhile, Bill's first picture, the fire story, began to show more widely, catching the eye of a reviewer at the *New York American*. ("It is harmless but enjoyable, like pictures in their early days, intending to be only an entertainment.") Bill believed the tide was turning. He worked around the clock on the sea story, making preparations.

Alice left her husband and moved into her sister's apartment on West 57th Street where Bill would often stay with her. Alice's sister, meanwhile, was in a sanitarium in Delaware with phobias.

Some evenings, they would dine with Alice's parents, who had a town house in the city. Bill found the dinners a chore. Her father, in his eighties, was a former banker who was thirty years older than his wife. His family, prominent in the city's Social Register, was descended from the first Dutch settlers of Manhattan. He clearly did not like his daughter's new profession, nor did he like Bill, refusing to talk to him on some visits but finding ways to insult him on others. ("I've never been to a flicker and I never will. It's no better than vaudeville. I don't see why you two waste your time.")

When Alice told him the story of the sea picture, her father said, "Well, I wouldn't go see that. I wouldn't be interested in that. Sounds like slop to me."

He would spend every dinner either dozing between courses or talking about the kaiser and whether there would be a war. Bill despised him.

His contract with Longstreet had Bill financing

all pictures beyond the second from any revenue from the business. He continued to tell Longstreet they were making a profit when that was not the case, so he lacked the money to finish the third picture, the sea story. Alice had inherited money from her grandfather, enough of a sum to finance it on her own. She knew of Bill's financial problems, and he believed she would offer to step in. Without thinking, just to be polite, he said one night that he would find a way to pay for it himself, figuring she would overrule him. She did not, and once he said it, that was that.

Bill sold his Buick, watches, gold money clip, and whatever else of value he owned. The sea story, in its final form, was going to be four reels. He decided to film the difficult scenes first. With the weather forecast saying that a storm was approaching, he rented a two-masted schooner and its crew for three days. However, the ship had been taking meat between Florida and New York City, and it stank horribly. No one could last more than five minutes below decks.

To make matters worse, after money changed hands, the captain informed Bill that he would not go out in very bad weather, even though that was the very thing that was needed – shots taken as the ship rolled on high waves. The captain said he would only take it out when the waves were smaller than five feet.

Frustrated, Bill bought a barrel and cut it in two.

They put to sea with relatively calm waters. He placed the camera in a barrel half and rolled it back and forth to give the effect of rolling seas, using up a whole day and two reels of film, with Alice and his bodyguards playing out their parts. The film was unusable. The barrel rolled, but the ship, the actors, and the sea did not. It looked only like an unsteady camera.

In her sister's apartment that evening, Alice informed Bill she was going back to her husband, that they had talked through their differences. Bill was furious. They argued violently and he broke a valuable mirror. Alice ordered him to leave, threatening to call the police. Bill dared her to. ("Let's see how that will look in the papers.") She got a steely look in her eyes and lifted the telephone. He left.

The next morning, Bill called Longstreet, confessing that he had run out of money. Again Longstreet had the tone of a disinterested bystander.

"Why, that's awful. What do you think you'll do now, Bill?"

"Can you lend me the funds to finish?"

Longstreet said he would not be able to do that. "A business has a natural life. I don't believe in extending it if the fates say its end has come. Let it die, Bill. Let it come to its natural end. You're to be commended for the effort."

Frantic, Bill began soliciting investors, sending

letters to names culled from the *New York Times* business page. He mentioned John D. Rockefeller's interest in "moral films," something that he read in the *Times*. When he received funds from a retired railroad man based on the claim, he only enhanced it.

"Mr. Rockefeller, who is one of the investors, sees the highly moral motion pictures we plan to make as the entertainment future, and so should you."

After raising seven thousand dollars within weeks, he finished the picture using another actress, filming the ocean scenes on a set. A wheelhouse was built on heavy automobile springs so that it could be rocked with wooden planks. A fire hose provided the sea spray. Long shots of boats in New York Harbor, taken from Battery Park when the seas were rough, set the scene.

In three weeks, *Sea of Sorrows* was finished, but as Bill prepared to sell it, he found the theatres even less willing to take independent films than they had been. His exchange friend was able to book it into one theatre in Mount Vernon. Concerned that it would fail, Bill told no one of the premiere, attending on his own. The theatre was half full. Some walked out before it ended. In the lobby afterward, Bill asked an elderly woman whether she enjoyed it, saying he was thinking of going inside for the next showing.

"A waste of your money," she said.

Days later, Bill was arrested at the warehouse by postal inspectors, who accused him of fraud. He immediately thought of the false prospectus, the claims about Rockefeller's interest. He spent the night in the Tombs Prison, listening to the wheezing and coughing of the inmates around him. In the depths of the night, he began sobbing quietly, sure his life could go no lower and sure it would never again go any higher. He considered hanging himself in the cell and actually stood on his bunk in the dark to feel for an overhead water pipe from which to commit the act. He found none. Lying back on his bunk, he settled again into his misery and slept.

However, his arrest proved to have been a mistake. At noon the next day, a postal inspector informed him that Longstreet and various associates in New York and other cities had been arrested, that Longstreet himself was being held elsewhere in the jail. The inspector said that an examination of Longstreet's accounting books showed Bill had not been involved in the fraud.

"They swindled small industrial corporations by offering to sell their securities on the English market," the inspector told him. "They never did, but they sure as anything collected all the fees they said the English charged."

Later, Bill would learn that from the very beginning Longstreet had a buyer in line to purchase the warehouse and all the equipment, a South American who himself was interested in making films. Longstreet had written the contract with Bill so that he would profit either way, whether Bill succeeded or failed.

20.

Marion and the physician

Despondent and lonely, Marion began to read the Bible intently in her spare time. If she had a little more courage ("or less courage, whatever it takes," she confided to her friend at the library), she would have killed herself, but then the friend told her, "I've got someone for you."

She introduced Marion to a doctor from New Britain, south of Hartford. He had recently lost his wife to a cancer and had three young children. Marion first met them at church on a Sunday morning, immediately feeling part of the family, even though the doctor, of Irish and Austrian descent, was nearly twice her age, in his late thirties. She was twenty. ("All that living and you're only how old?" he remarked.)

On the last warm day of the fall, with a few sprigs of butter-and-eggs still blooming on the roadsides, they took the train to Manhattan. The doctor was intent on showing her the poor beginnings around Tompkins Square from which he had risen. Stopping by a pavilion in the square to watch old German and Israelite men playing chess, he told Marion that his parents were anarchists, that his father went to jail and never returned, dying of dysentery. He said he had marched proudly as a young boy, waving a black flag in a funeral parade on Tenth Avenue to protest the executions in Chicago after the Haymarket Affair. When he was eleven, his destitute mother sent him to live with middle-class relatives in Connecticut. With an intellect driven by brooding anger, he excelled in high school, then college, then medical school.

They walked down Avenue A, past the Church of the Holy Redeemer, with its bullet-shaped spire, to Corlears Park on the lower East Side, a desolate place of few trees. Beggars pleaded for nickels. Stray cats wandered about. In the East River, a rotting steamboat was tied to the wharf, with flowers adorning its upper deck and sickly, immobile people on its lower deck – the neighborhood's tuberculosis patients.

Here, Marion told the doctor of the early death of her father, then of her impoverishment growing up. When she told of her short, failed marriage to Bill, she turned to the doctor to measure the possible fatal disapproval in his eyes. A divorced woman. He was sympathetic, though. ("Was Bill a drunkard? Did he beat you?") Marion saw the genuine concern of a physician for any suffering person. They took a taxi to Battery Park on the tip of Manhattan as dusk approached, then watched in silent appreciation as the lights of New Jersey and Brooklyn blinked through the settling harbor haze.

Within weeks, the doctor spoke of his desire to marry her, and she spoke of her gratitude for his interest. She did not mention love; she could not. She was not sure she felt it, but she was also not sure that was altogether a bad sign. Marion considered deeper love, the sort that led to long marriages, a more complicated and less obvious emotion than what she had felt for Bill, which, to her thinking now, had been no more than the suffocating, indistinct yearning of a young girl.

Through the winter they met each Saturday, going to dinner and then the theatre, and on Sunday, with the children, they attended church. To the other doctors, he would proudly introduce her as "Marion Fiske, the screen actress." In January, during a snowstorm, he formally proposed and she accepted. The wedding was set for April of 1914.

With her optimism and vibrancy fully returned, Marion decided to write Bill with the news, feeling it not only proper but also a necessary ending to a chapter in her life. She sent the letter to the last address in Manhattan that she had for him. It was a month before he wrote back. His letter had a

Brooklyn address. As she slit open the envelope, she was angry at herself for feeling the anticipation that she did. Her heart fairly pounded.

The letter, in a poor pen, was only one paragraph long. A smudge of ink, perhaps Bill's fingerprint, was below his signature.

> Dear Marion,
> I'm glad things are going your way. You deserve all the best. May you be happy in your marriage and all your future endeavers. I am also about to be remarried. My wife to be is in the theatre. I hope you will soon know the joy of children.
> Your friend always,
> Bill

21.

The streets of Brooklyn

What once had been the music of New York, the constant and varied sounds of the city, was now, in the night, a terrible cacophony of noise to Bill. Sleep had become his chief enemy.

In May of 1914, he lived with his wife and baby in a tenement on Lafayette Avenue in Brooklyn, near the Prince Theatre, one of the new moving-picture palaces. He was the night manager of the theatre, which meant he had to sleep until late in the morning. His child, a son just a month old, had arrived during a marriage that was only two months old itself.

As Bill tried to sleep, all noise became small darts of sound intended to prick him just as the fog of sleep descended. The more he thought about the noise, the more aware of it he became, and once conscious of it, of each clack and clomp and sputter and whistle, he found he could not become unconscious of it, because that would take a deliberate effort, and making such an effort would only make him more conscious of it. The noise was at its worst as he tried to sleep after the sun rose and the commerce of the city came awake. There was the clatter of wagon wheels over cobblestone streets, the rumble of heavy trucks loaded with steel or iron girders destined for new office buildings, the jangle of cowbells on junk carts, the pounding of coal falling from coal wagons down building chutes, the scissors grinders, umbrella vendors, and newspaper hawkers with leather lungs and rowdy voices on the sidewalk, the horns of the ubiquitous automobiles, the clang of trolley bells, and the constant rattle of a great many kinds of machines in the nearby manufacturing districts, producing a great many different noises. In the tenements, his and others, there were the crying babies, the squealing children, and the argumentative voices of husbands and wives in constant dispute. Yet with ventilation so poor, he had no choice in warm weather but to throw open the windows, beckoning this din into his bedroom.

Before his marriage, Bill was burdened with debts related to the failure of his film company, which the court ordered him to repay. He was forced to seek steady work. However, the day of the one-reeler was all but gone – motion pictures had progressed rapidly – and his and many other recognizable names of 1911 had faded from prominence. As he searched for roles on stage or in films, he was but one in a huge crowd of actors doing the same.

Needing to pay his debts, he took a job as a teller at the Windsor Trust Company in Manhattan. One morning when he reported to work, police detectives were in the bank investigating the disappearance of ten thousand dollars from the lockboxes kept in a barred room behind the tellers' cages. Even though Bill did not have access to the boxes, he was interrogated longer than all the others because he had just started on the job.

A reward was offered in the case, and his name, Charles Trowbridge (he used his middle name for employment that embarrassed him), was published in the *New York American* as a suspect. Although detectives said they believed him innocent, Bill was convinced that for weeks men interested in the reward were following him, apparently to see if he would start spending large sums of money. Eventually, the cash was found in a hollow lamp of the bank's vice president during a search of his residence by detectives.

Bill stopped at a bathhouse one evening after work. He was in the steam room when men broke in and robbed the patrons. They ordered everyone into the locker room. Bill said something under his breath about the cold floors, and a robber, who apparently did not speak English, took it that it was something being said about his mutilated ear. He beat Bill with a blackjack, opening a gash requiring thirty-two stitches. At the hospital, a doctor thought he was treating one of the robbers, and his inattention left Bill with an ugly scar on his forehead, caused by infection. The sight of it prevented him from considering any acting roles, and he spent anxious nights applying different formulations of makeup until he found one that could conceal it.

Bill was eventually able to get the job at the Prince Theatre, a position that he thought might give him the business experience to return one day to some aspect of filmmaking. It was during this time that he met his wife, a dancer in the Ziegfeld Follies at the New Amsterdam Theatre. He had wined and dined some of the Ziegfeld girls before. In this instance, a pregnancy intervened to bring on a wedding.

The Prince Theatre on Fulton Street had once made its money showing "white slave" films, movies that offered "the true story of the abduction of daughters and wives into the world of prostitution," the movie posters proclaimed. However, police raids and court injunctions brought the theatre to financial ruin. A new, magnificent theatre was built in its place, but this only made Bill's misery worse, since the better films the house now showed were the very types of films he aspired to make. Night after night, he would stand at the back of the theatre, muttering under his breath at the perceived shortcomings of what was on the screen.

He was in Manhattan one afternoon to pick up that evening's films from an exchange when he recognized Charles Blanchard on Canal Street. Charles was noticeably thinner, his eyes less clear, his hair graying. Bill was, in fact, excited to to see him, since it revived for him the memory of happier times. They chatted on the sidewalk. Charles was in New York to see brokers and bankers. The brothers now owned department stores in the Midwest. Bill said he owned a motion-picture theatre but was dissatisfied with that end of the business.

"Why don't you get back into acting?" Charles asked.

"It's not that easy. I'm married these days and I've got a family."

"So some girl finally caught you for good."

"To tell you the truth, I caught myself. A baby came along, so that has really settled me down," Bill said with humility.

"Do I know your wife?"

"She was a dancer. She was with Ziegfeld at the New Amsterdam. Imogene Kirk."

"You sure she wasn't a Fielding girl?"

"A Ziegfeld girl. She did it a couple of years."

"That's good. In the Fielding Follies, the girls

were naked. They did their show on the roof of a place on Broadway. At the start, the girls wore balloons that you would burst with your cigar when they came around to your table. So by the end of the night, they were in the altogether."

"A Ziegfeld girl, Charles."

"I'm kidding you."

"I'll tell you, though, this business of running other people's movies, it drives me crazy. I see what passes for motion pictures these days, the cheap stuff these studios put out, and it makes me sick."

"It's a different world," Charles said wistfully.

"Blanchard Brothers did some of the best stuff yet. What really makes me sick, though, is I think of what actors are making today. I heard Williams, what's his name, Earle Williams, a nobody, is getting three hundred dollars a year, and Mabel Normand . . ."

"You mean a week."

"Yeah, three hundred a week. And Mabel Normand, who's no great actress, she's getting five hundred. There's nothing special about them. Half the actors today haven't even heard of Blanchard Brothers. They don't know what we contributed to this business. We were the pioneers, you and I."

Charles nodded agreement but seemed to be looking for an opportunity to escape.

"Look," Bill said. "I heard someone smart patented the sprocket holes on the film, the process for punching them as the film goes through the camera. Someone holds the patent to that."

"Edison probably."

"Well, we did a picture, *Their Hearts Were Young*. Remember that? And I did a little two-step I invented, a little dance, and it became very popular. I read someone got a crowd of people doing it in a dance hall in Albany. Now, couldn't I patent that so actors would have to pay me to do it?"

"Oh, I'm sure people did that on stage. Every kind of dance has been done on stage."

"Yes, but it was the first time on film. I'm sure people put holes in things before but someone patented it when they put holes in film."

"Maybe."

"If I'd saved copies of my films, I'd go through them and find all the things I did first. Maybe I was the first actor in motion pictures to laugh in a certain way. Maybe I held my sides when I laughed. So maybe I invented that particular laugh. If I had four or five of these things, I bet I could find a lawyer and get a patent. What do you think?"

22.

The wedding party

The story in the *New York Times* said that Miss Josephine Price Pincney had committed suicide by swallowing carbolic acid on the golf links at the Sunnyside Golf Club in Albany. Estelle read the account while on a train between New York and Baltimore. A touring stage company she owned, billed as "Movie Players in Plays," was on its spring tour in Maryland, where she was to join it.

Following the closing of Blanchard Brothers, Estelle had moved to Vitagraph in Brooklyn, where she made a dozen films before going to the West Coast in 1914. She consistently found work in Hollywood and came to be regarded as one of the foremost character actresses in motion pictures. Hers was, said one magazine, "The face you know, the name you do not."

In San Francisco, just for fun, she recruited lesser-known film actors, all between jobs, for a one-week run of the play *A Visit to Tulip Lane*. She could have sold enough tickets to fill the rented theatre five times over. As a result, she formed two traveling companies of actors, who came and went as their motion-picture work allowed. Vacancies were filled from a waiting list of others between jobs. Their success was enormous, and there were sellouts almost wherever they appeared. Estelle, without any intention, became not only wealthy but revered in her industry for the opportunities she gave marginal actors and actresses.

Now, though, in March of 1916, aboard a railroad passenger car an hour outside Baltimore, she read of the suicide. Not that she knew Miss Pincney. She did not. However, she knew of her kind. Miss Josephine Price Pincney was, Estelle gathered, in her middle years and unmarried. The *Times* said she was an heiress and had visited the home in Albany of her younger sister, Mrs. Walter Hyde, and played with her sister's children before her visit to the golf links. Estelle wondered how many people would read the *Times* and say, "What could possibly cause a woman of means to do that?"

Estelle knew. Suicide for people in their later years was about illness. For young people, it was about confusion. However, for people in their middle years, it was about disappointment. Miss

Pincney had not gotten what she wanted in life, what she was convinced with all her being that she deserved. From birth, Estelle believed, women had an expectation of what is deserved: a place, a situation, a level of happiness, a husband perhaps, and children. It is so fundamental in one's beliefs that when this expectation is unfulfilled, suicide seems acceptable, even logical.

Life had abandoned her, Miss Pincney must have decided. The acid, the emphasis created by the conspicuous location of a golf course: these things said exactly that. She was angry at life, angry enough to end her connection to it in a way that would be written about in the *Times*. The act would be a public affront to life. It would say, "See? Here's an example of the unhappiness that life creates. All be warned: have no expectations."

Estelle was traveling from New York City with little sleep. The night before, nearly twenty thousand people had overflowed Madison Square Garden for the Suffrage Ball. The great building was draped inside with blue, yellow, and white bunting as well as American flags. John Philip Sousa's band played and the Hippodrome Ballet entertained. Estelle, a major contributor to the cause, joined sixty or so of the most recognizable names in the national movement during the grand march down the hall late in the evening, accompanied by the exuberant cheering and clapping of the massive crowd.

Yet now, reading of this suicide, she felt an inconsolable sadness for a woman she did not even know. Estelle had once visited Sunnyside Golf Club, the guest of a member and his wife. They had a lunch of shrimp and oysters in the clubhouse. Estelle tried to imagine where Miss Pincney chose to commit her act. Would she have sought isolation, perhaps a green carved out of deep woods? Or would she have sought a public spot, a hill in the middle of a wide fairway with a commanding view of Albany?

Estelle sighed heavily, suddenly feeling weary. She closed her eyes and absorbed the regular shaking of the train and the monotonous sounds of its movement over the rails. Estelle knew that what she really felt was loneliness. Loneliness had been her regular companion lately. It was with her in a way it had never been in the previous five years. Since losing Bill, she had not met another man for whom she felt any spark of authentic feeling. Those she met seemed to stay only peripheral to her, like a comet or meteor traveling close to Earth's atmosphere but ultimately passing by. However, she had been so occupied with her career and her politics that she never missed such a presence in her life – until now.

Baltimore, Washington, Richmond, Knoxville, Indianapolis. Estelle's eastern company had three plays it could choose from, depending on the number and gender of its players at any given moment. The cast turned over frequently as the actors and actresses found film work, replacements being sent out to meet the tour through a central office in Los Angeles.

Howard Drew joined the company in Indianapolis, his first experience with them. He had most recently worked for Essanay Films. He was forty-one, with an amiable face, large ears, and a mouth that seemed to be perpetually smiling. Like Estelle, he had begun in theatre as a juvenile, attaining a starring role on Broadway when he was only nine in *The Boy Who Became a Prince*. It closed within weeks, he told Estelle, and he had not starred again in any play or film. ("My appearance changed in such a way that precluded the necessary audience sympathies," he said self-mockingly.) Married at nineteen, he was divorced at twenty-one and had been a self-described contented bachelor since.

To Estelle, he seemed kind and affable, the qualities that seemed to come across in his films. That image had earned him a secure place in motion pictures as a character actor.

He met the rest of the company at the Star Theatre in Indianapolis five hours before the curtain. They were doubtful of his claim that he had fully learned the lines and blocking on the train, and they were prepared to substitute a different play – until he recited not only his lines but all others from the opening scenes.

After a nearly flawless performance and a standing ovation, the company went to a late supper at a local restaurant. Estelle listened as Howard told stories about Charlie Chaplin and others at Essanay. She thought his voice kind, his words graceful and diplomatic. With Chaplin's popularity and exorbitant salary, it was common when actors gossiped to talk about his poor bathing habits and his disreputable interest in young girls. Howard mentioned none of this, instead complimenting the actor for the admirable way he handled his fame and obliged those who came up to him on the street.

Late in the evening, when he was speaking only with Estelle, she saw a tentative, uncertain look in his eyes, as if he were struggling to maintain composure. She knew she felt the same.

Estelle could not sleep that night, an unusual condition for her. She was to return to Hollywood to start a picture after their five-night run ended in Indianapolis, and a replacement for her was already en route. Lying in bed, she felt an urgency to her thoughts. The surrounding noise of the hotel, the occasional cough from other rooms, the footsteps in the hallway, and the auto horns from outside all seemed magnified. She thought about the evening and about Howard, realizing that even though she had spent the past ten hours with him, she could not clearly recall what he looked like. Yet his soft voice was in her mind as if it were a recording playing on a phonograph.

The urgency of the moment pressed at her, as did her loneliness. Its meaning to her became undeniable. She began to scheme about ways to remain with the company, and soon she felt a peace of mind and the approach of sleep.

She telephoned her Los Angeles office in the morning and had her replacement rerouted to the western company, which was in Phoenix. Then she called the director of the film she was about to begin. Up until the moment he answered the telephone, she was ready to plead sickness but worried that he would not believe such a typical excuse. So instead she blurted out the truth.

"I've met a man and I'm forty years old and it's more important."

The director laughed, then genuinely wished her luck and happiness.

Three months later, in Seattle's Trinity Parish Episcopal Church, Estelle and Howard were married in front of two hundred guests, including Mary Pickford.

23.

Dancing atop the Biltmore

The fashion in the summer of 1917 in Manhattan was for dancing on the open roofs of the city's fine hotels: the Biltmore, the Ritz-Carlton, the McAlpin, the Astor. The cool breezes caressed the couples on sultry July evenings, a dreamy diversion from the European war.

America had entered the war that April. Trying to stay clear of the great conflict had proved impossible. Two years earlier, the Germans had sunk the passenger ship *Lusitania*, supposedly uninvolved in the conflict, as it crossed the Atlantic from New York to Liverpool. Scores of Americans were killed and the drumbeat for the fight began. A later investigation would show that the ship's hull had in fact been filled with weapons to be used by the British against Germany, including four million rounds of Remington rifle cartridges disguised as bales of fur and boxes of cheese.

Bill, still a theatre manager in Brooklyn, learned to ignore the war news, for it made him more tired and unhappy than he already was.

One afternoon, while in Manhattan to buy theatre supplies, he met a girl along Broadway and, on a whim, took her dancing that evening. His wife and son were waiting for him at home, expecting him to return for dinner.

The way he met the girl, to him, seemed a small destiny. He passed a new apartment building, the Sanford and Rexford, up Broadway at 78th Street. A sign stationed on the sidewalk said, "high-class apartments open for inspection." Interested in seeing what his money, if he had been able to retain any of it, would have rented, he joined a tour. An attractive young woman and her parents, or so he thought, were also on the tour. They fell into conversation as freshly painted windows and closet doors were opened and closed. The man asked Bill if he planned to fight in France. He said he did and would soon be called up. In fact, Bill had failed the physical for the draft because of the diminishment of his eyesight caused by the bathhouse beating.

The man, a Christian Scientist from Illinois, was visiting the city to address the General Federation of Women's Clubs. He was director of the American Society of Hygiene. From the way he never left the topic, his obsession appeared to be wayward girls who fell into the evil embrace of the city.

"This is my first visit to New York, although I have been to Paris," he said. "You go to Paris only to marvel at the prices and to see all the strange people. Young girls are as susceptible there as here in New York. Both cities are renowned for seducing them into vice."

Bill glanced at the daughter, whom he judged to be about eighteen. He saw her intolerant look and knew everything. Having to listen to her father's condemning views day after day had forged a nascent contempt in her. He enjoyed seeing it. He despised men like her father, supposed guardians of good. Instead, he saw true goodness in their daughters' contempt for them.

"Now, I've done a study," the man said. "Not a small minority of wayward girls come from good and decent homes, I imagine. They are daughters of respectable men, although it's fair to say the majority are ignorant and poor, with no concept of right and wrong."

The daughter said it was actually negligent parents who drove such girls to do what they did, confusing Bill with her accusatory tone toward her father.

"That's not true," the man said. "That was part of my study. Such girls share certain characteristics. They are rebellious against their parents, negligent or not, and they are suspicious and scornful of their boyfriends."

The girl laughed as if she thought his conclusions ridiculous.

"Where are your parents, young lady?" the wife asked her sternly.

Bill now realized that things were not as they seemed.

"Why, that's none of your business," the girl said.

"It *is* my business. It's the business of every good person that can act in the place of parents to girls on their own such as you."

The girl smiled as she would have at a zoo on seeing a monkey do something particularly amusing – the smile of one who knows she is not of the same species as what she is viewing.

"Well, young lady, where are your parents?" the woman asked again.

"They died of stupidity. I should warn you, just before they went, they had some of the same symptoms as you have."

With that, she turned and walked out of the apartment. Bill followed her, intent on congratulating her for her well-aimed comments.

"That was a great thing. Absolutely great. They deserved it," he told her.

On the sidewalk, walking down Broadway, they fell into a comfortable conversation. Not intending to brag, just providing a statement of information, Bill told her about his early cinema career, his failed attempt to start his own studio, and his current life of retribution. ("I live alone in Brooklyn, where I own a small movie house.")

It was the kind of story you might hear in all quarters of the city as cosmopolitan writers, artists, and others briefly stated their life story to new acquaintances. However, it turned out the girl had just arrived from Ohio and was staying at the YMCA adjunct hotel for women. She said she had never heard such a glamorous story. She said this was her first encounter with an element of New York that had drawn her to the city in the first place: its artists. Bill said he was greatly complimented.

They walked and talked for nearly an hour with no particular destination – with, in fact, the deliberate destination of no destination as if to emphasize the wonderful encounter in which they were involved. It was as if they were both thinking, "Let us agree to lose our sense of ourselves, of time, of familiar habits. Lovers lose them. We are losing them, don't you see?"

In front of the Hotel Biltmore, they saw a sign: "Roof now open for dancing and dining each evening." It was closed at the moment, the time being only five o'clock. So instead they took tea on the lower roof that fronted Vanderbilt Avenue. Here, in a reproduction of an Italian garden, beneath striped umbrellas, they drank and talked, relating details of their childhoods and the strange odysseys that had brought them to New York.

Later, hearing orchestra music from above, they went to investigate but found themselves in a throng of people on the stairway trying to reach the rooftop. Cards were required, and having none, they prepared to leave when a voice called out, "Billy Trowbridge!" It was Emil Fries, the former manager at the Hood's Theatre on Broadway, where so many of Bill's pictures had premiered. Emil was now an assistant manager at the Biltmore. He insisted they be allowed to pass by the line to the roof.

It was another small example of destiny, Bill thought, a continuing conspiracy of events. The wonderful young girl, the recognition of him as a cinema star, the dancing atop the Biltmore – it all came together now to remind him of his privileged former life. Suddenly, he felt its loss sharply. He knew he could no longer stand the life he had, a wife he did not love, a troublesome child, his slavery to an industry he should have ruled as a star. It was now unbearable. It had always been unbearable, but the habit of bearing it had made it seem otherwise, he realized.

By midnight, dancing beside the rooftop waterfall, this beautiful girl in his arms, all of New York spread in lights around him, he knew he would never go back to Brooklyn except to collect his clothes, arrange as best he could for his family's financial stability, and then leave.

He stayed free in a room at the Biltmore that night, courtesy of Emil. Bill's only act of chivalry was to urge the girl to return to the YMCA and not stay with him. The following morning, he contacted his former vaudeville booking agent, now acting as agent for the stage productions of Wheeler and Stolle. He got Bill a role in the touring company of *History's Villains*, playing John Wilkes Booth.

In Syracuse a week later, Bill appeared from behind a side curtain in the presidential box, brandished his single-shot derringer, took the infamous shot, and then, with enthusiastic boos from the crowd, leaped to the stage, shouting, "*sic semper tyrannis!*"

24.

Chatting in the cemetery

Just after Thanksgiving in the fourth year of her marriage, Marion recognized the signs that she was pregnant. She cried with joy.

As her figure subtly expanded in succeeding weeks, she began to feel a connection to the baby within her that was deeper and more personal than what she felt for her husband's children, even though she loved them dearly. They had been well past infancy when she married, the youngest nearly five. So this baby would carry a world with it that Marion had not lived in since she was a child herself, a wondrous world more authentic for its unguarded emotions and sincere enthusiasms. To show this child flowers, books, horses, and snow for the first time would be to see them as she had first seen them as a child. She experienced a nervous elation anticipating the birth.

Marion passed the winter preparing the nursery and reading all the manuals on motherhood she could find. Advised to rest each afternoon, she spent her spare time while the children were at school reading the movie fan magazines her daughter had begun buying, poring over the stories, getting dreamy about the stars of the modern cinema and the luxurious lives they lived in California.

However, in January, she experienced severe cramps and bleeding that put her in bed for days. Her husband did not tell her immediately that he feared she had lost the baby. However, she dreamed of the baby's death and awoke convinced of it. An examination confirmed the fact and also suggested she might never have children.

She felt her life to be at such a low ebb, her spirit so diminished, that she believed it within her power to will her own death. Only her husband's constant attention and comforting words brought her through.

Marion received a letter from the wife of Harold Baines, an actor she had met when working for Blanchard Brothers. He had filled in for Bill at the studio during three days that Bill was sick, the result of heavy drinking. Harold later moved to California and worked for the Hal Roach studio.

Marion became friends with his wife, who had been on the set those few days in New Jersey. They continued to correspond once or twice a year and visited in Manhattan after the couple moved back east. The letter said Harold had died and that there was to be a funeral at a church in Pelham, north of New York City, with burial in the adjoining cemetery. She hoped Marion could attend since so few motion-picture people who knew her husband lived around the city. Still mourning, Marion would not have gone had it not been for this personal request.

Arriving at the church late, she sat in a rear pew. As the organ music played, a woman in a hooded cloak came in and sat beside her. When she removed the hood, Marion realized it was Lillian Gish, the Biograph star, as famous at that moment as anyone in films. With her heart pounding, Marion leaned over and boldly introduced herself as a former actress at Blanchard Brothers, "one of the early film companies in New Jersey."

"Marion Fiske?" Lillian said, her face suddenly alight with recognition. "Why, I know your name very well."

Before her start at Biograph, Lillian and her sister were stage actresses in New York City and loved going to movies during the day, she said. One of their favorites was *The Bride of Battle*. Now Lillian was back in New York, preparing to work on a film, and she was renting an apartment in Manhattan with her mother. Wistfully, she talked about her small-town Ohio upbringing and how "New York is so full of it."

Later, waiting in the cemetery for the burial to begin, the two stood apart from the crowd for a time, continuing to talk about the movies' early days, the excitement and the difficulties, the scorching lights and poor wages, but also the more genuine friendships. Lillian talked at length about the transition of motion pictures to California and the increasing intrusion of business into films. Still feeling a bit awed, Marion talked about the steady contentment of married life but of the loss of the stimulation that acting had created.

Home in Connecticut that night, Marion brushed her hair before the dressing table mirror, telling her husband of the experience, still feeling excitement and pride at having been remembered by someone as famous as Lillian Gish.

"Listening to her, I have to say, I found myself slipping into the movie-fan frame of mind. I was a bit tongue-tied, especially as she talked so familiarly about people I'd only read about – D. W. Griffith and Pearl White."

Marion turned to her husband, who lay in bed reading. "It's an odd thing. Here, for a short while, I saw movie fame from the other side, so you'd think I would be immune to its lure, but I'm not. You would think I'd been cured. I used to read stories about the English kings and what people put up with in that country with their royalty. Being an American, I thought, well, it's all just insanity. Who would allow themselves to think of this duke or duchess as better than themselves, as someone who was more of a deserving person? But they did. What stupid people the English were. But here I'd once been royalty of the screen. And still, with that experience, knowing exactly what stupidity any worship of such people is, here I was thinking the very same thing about Lillian. It made me understand; the English had no chance. There's nothing in a human being capable of overcoming this particular kind of stupidity."

"You ought to act again," her husband said. "Some of the club women in Hartford have a theatre group, you know. They put on plays to raise money for the settlement house."

Marion continued brushing her hair, examining her face in the mirror, wondering if it might ever recover the glow it once had on the screen.

"I don't know if I remember how."

"You'd remember. Talent is a natural gift. It's always there."

25.

Bill as the pugilist

The circumstances that returned Bill Trowbridge to movies involved a bet. On the afternoon of July 4, 1919, the country's attention was on a boxing ring in Toledo, Ohio, where Jess Willard, the "man mountain" from Kansas, who was also the heavyweight champion, lost the title to the relatively unknown Jack Dempsey, with Willard's seconds throwing in the sponge at the fourth-round bell.

In San Francisco, still playing John Wilkes Booth for the Wheeler and Stolle touring company, Bill awaited the fight results via telegraph at the hall of the Knights of Columbus. So confident was he that Willard would emerge the victor that he made a wager with a boastful Marine from the city's training station, a Dempsey man who claimed to be an ex-fighter. The loser would roll a peanut down Van Ness Avenue with his nose a distance of a quarter mile.

A crowd, including a photographer from the *Examiner*, surrounded Bill as he began his payment. After only a block, he appealed to the Marine for mercy, saying the sidewalk was rough on his nose and his knees were too tender. The Marine, obviously drunk, scolded Bill, prodding him on in a humiliating fashion with his foot. An argument ensued, with the Marine threatening to give Bill "all that Willard got." Bill rose from the ground at that point, and with a single battering ram of a punch, he dropped the Marine, breaking his jaw.

It was learned afterward that the Marine was the former holder of a Utah ring title. The *Examiner* ran Bill's picture alongside that of a scowling Dempsey, there being some resemblance. "Actor also a boxer," the caption read.

Three weeks later, a Los Angeles agent telephoned Bill in Emporia, Kansas, where the villains' tour had taken him. He said he could get him the lead in a boxing picture, *The Pugilists*.

"The film is about a brutal but likable fighter, who is you, in the control of criminal element. He is finally beaten by an honest hero."

"Why can't I play the honest hero?"

"It's you who's the star. You smile at the young fighter at the end, even though you're defeated, and that wins you back the audience."

Steel-Warde Films was the studio. ("No one's heard of them, because they're up in Ventura," the agent explained.) The salary offered was two thousand dollars. Bill was on a train to California the next morning. The movie was shot in Montecito by the ocean. He was paid only six hundred dollars by the studio, with a promise of the rest once the film was in theatres. With two weeks left in the shooting, though, the studio's creditors forced the company into bankruptcy and the court impounded the still unedited footage. Bill was told he would likely never get the remainder of his salary.

Through the same agent, who said he felt responsible for Bill's predicament, he was able to find steady but poorly paid work as an extra, often as a thug in gangster pictures. Bill told the agent he was capable of better parts, even leading man roles.

"Character actors are all you'll ever play. You don't have the face," the agent said bluntly.

This shocked Bill, who still retained a remnant of pride in having been "the handsomest man in pictures." He believed it was only through bad luck that he was out of movies and had lost the title.

He had taken a room in a lodging house in Mar Vista in west Los Angeles. In his trunk, among his photographs, was the one publicity shot he had left from his Blanchard Brothers days. He stood before the mirror and examined himself and the picture.

Owing to years of jumping on to stages as Booth, he had persistent back pain, so he no longer could exercise daily. As a result, he was heavier by thirty pounds. Yes, some of that extra weight appeared in his face, he acknowledged, and yes, his intermittent insomnia had put bags beneath his eyes and wrinkles around them, and yes, his hairline was not where it once had been. However, many leading men showed experience in their looks. Women did not like plain-faced, simple men. They liked to see men who had been through something, who had gained some wisdom and complication. The studios had it wrong. He had more in him than criminals, tramps, and roustabouts.

Angry, he vowed to get himself into shape. He found a doctor who prescribed laudanum for his back pain. This enabled him to swim and tan on the beach at Venice on his days off. In his room in the evenings, he lifted dumbbells. Within weeks, he saw a dramatic change in his appearance, a subtraction of years from the mirror. He grew determined to reestablish a proper place for himself in movies. However, his agent seemed just as determined to keep him in character roles, telling him the studios were not interested in him for anything else. Suspecting the agent was lying, he went to another agent, who told him most of the same things.

"The studios want you to be a certain kind of handsome, and you're not that kind, although you're not really that bad-looking," he said.

Bill took what roles he could find, but when not working, he would stay in his rented room drinking for days. He regained much of the lost weight.

Months earlier, while on the road in Indiana, he had received a letter from a friend in Brooklyn giving the first news of his family in two years. It offered belated condolences for the death of his son in the influenza epidemic, and it also gave details of his wife's remarriage to a theatrical promoter shortly after the boy's death. Bill was unaware of either of these events and had continued to pay both alimony – they had divorced in 1917 – and child support to his wife, as ordered by the court. On getting the letter, he considered bringing fraud charges against her, but did not.

Now, though, he paced in his room in Mar Vista drinking Barber's gin. He went through his trunk for family photographs and found one he had of his son as a baby. He was in a carriage on DeKalb Avenue in Brooklyn. A neighborhood German shepherd, called Mike the Comet, was standing with his paws up on the carriage, peering at the boy. A street photographer snapped the picture for ten cents.

It was past midnight and Bill stood at the window to put the available street light on the photo. He suddenly missed his son as he never had in life, and he felt the weight of his own mistakes and misfortunes as he never had before.

26.

A waiter's errand

Estelle was appearing in a film with Mary Pickford, being shot at Mary's studio on Formosa Avenue in Hollywood. Around noon, a message was passed to Estelle on the set. It said Bill Trowbridge was at the gate and requested lunch, "if you can find the time for an old friend."

Estelle had difficulty concentrating as the rehearsal finished. The last time she had seen Bill was 1912. Seven years. She asked the makeup woman to fix her hair and she borrowed better clothes from the costume department.

As she approached the gate, she did not immediately recognize him. The man in the suit and boater, a bit stocky, with a weathered face, was an agent or business manager perhaps. It was only when he waved that she realized who it was.

Estelle made every attempt to hide her astonishment at his appearance as they hugged. This was not the same Bill, she thought. He looked now like an ordinary middle-aged man.

As they walked to a nearby restaurant, they talked about the intervening years, about Estelle's marriage, Bill's failed second marriage ("Will I ever get it right?"), the war, the armistice, the passage of the suffrage amendment in the Senate. However, a lesson began to settle into her thinking. Over the next hour, she would decide that someone like Bill could only be admired in youth. They did not have the character to surmount the process of aging. There would be nothing pushing from inside that, later in life, would make the outside appear to be more than what it was. She would think of her husband, a decade older than Bill. He was not attractive in the traditional way, yet he had a strange peacefulness about him, a kindliness that made people smile and wish to be around him. He had become pleasing to look at in a way Bill had not.

Now, waiting for a table in the restaurant, Bill said he had enjoyed some success on the stage and was only recently coaxed back into movies with a starring role in a boxing picture that was soon to premiere.

"To be honest, I'm between jobs right now, but I read you've got a part in Mary Pickford's latest film. Good for you. Any chance there might be something for me?"

"I'm sorry to say it's all been cast. Mary has her players that she likes to use. Sorry, Bill."

"Well, if they need extras, I'd do it – not because I need the money. I have some offers. It's just, you know, the great honor of working with Mary Pickford . . . and to work with you again, of course."

Once seated, Bill ordered a beer even before he ordered his sandwich, something that made Estelle nervous – men whose priority at lunch was drinking. They talked about the state of motion pictures. A second beer eventually launched Bill into a monologue on the death of dreams.

"My theory is this," he said. "People are desperate because they have no dreams anymore, and motion pictures are the reason. Movies have shown them how life really is, how people really are. They've seen what fools politicians and people like that are. They know that the rich aren't happy . . ."

"The rich aren't happy?"

"You know what I mean, and people've seen how most men don't stand a chance at all against all the big money men. They've seen this all in movies. So what's the point of living anymore? Dreams and believing things are good, that people are good, that you have a chance in the world, are the only things that make you wake up each day, and once you realize how much a lie all that is, you don't want to wake up."

"It was the war, too," Estelle said.

"That's right. It was the war, too. Look. Here's something else. I'll tell you why I personally think the future is a bleak place. It's this idea of poison gas. From now on, poison gas is part of our daily lives. Every country has it, and no matter what they say, every country will use it. People can make it in basement laboratories. You can go out and buy the recipe. The inventor of it, a man from Berlin, he was in the papers last week bragging about how many people it can kill and how if only the German generals had let him make enough of it, he would have gassed France to death. He was *bragging*. He says we've only touched the possibilities of what chemicals can do to slaughter people. The underworld knows this, too. Bullets are ineffective. Poison gas is what they crave."

"I've never read this."

"Exactly. The government doesn't want you to know. Any day now, whole cities will be exterminated because the underworld wants the money in them. They'll kill everybody and clean out the valuables."

"Oh, come on, Bill."

"Honestly. Listen to this. This'll tell you about the government. Right now, you can't get a gold coin if you tried. Our money is backed with gold, but you can't go into a bank and obtain any kind of gold coin. You have to go down to the U.S. Treasury in Washington. They have to give you your coin because right on the bills it says it's gold-backed and it would cause a panic if the Treasury refused. But go into any local bank and ask for gold and they look at you like you're mad. Why? Because the government knows that what's coming is gas attacks on cities by the underworld. The United States has half the world's gold and it's all been locked up in special vaults where they wear gas masks all day."

"You mean if I walked across the street to the bank, I can't get a five-dollar gold piece?" Estelle said.

"That's exactly it. Exactly. But don't take my word for it." Bill summoned the maitre d'. "Excuse me, good sir. I'm wondering if someone in the kitchen who might be on a smoke break wants to earn two bits. Here's a five-dollar bill. Could someone go across the street there, to that bank, and get it exchanged for a gold piece, a half eagle?"

The man looked around. "Yes, we have someone who could do that."

"And if the bank says no, you have your man ask why."

"Certainly, sir."

Bill was growing more agitated. "Estelle, if people knew this, about gold being gone because of this gas thing, how do you think they'd feel? How much worse?"

"I think the answer is to get up, eat a good

breakfast, read the paper, take a walk, work in your garden. Enjoy moments for what they are. Enjoy the sunshine," she said.

"People aren't like you. All these things going on in the world affect them. They're driven to work for something up ahead in their lives, and I don't think there's anything ahead in the future but misery."

They ate in silence for a few minutes.

"Look," Bill said. "Here's why the crooks will turn to gas. I read something a few weeks ago. There were more than a hundred bank robberies in the United State last year, and you know how much they got in total? Guess."

"I don't know," Estelle said. "But just because you're asking, it can't be high. So . . . a half million."

"It was more than that but less than a million, less than some picture people make."

"Less than Chaplin."

"That's exactly right. Less than what Chaplin makes. Guns are no longer enough for the criminals. Gas is the next thing for them. Say, there's our fellow."

The waiter who had been sent came in from the street with the bill. "I'm sorry. The bank would not exchange it. They said there's no demand for gold coins except at Christmas, so they keep them in a vault the rest of the year."

"That's what they say, do they? Well, here's for

your trouble."

Bill handed the man a quarter, then he turned to Estelle. "See? It's happening. The government knows what this gas is going to become in our lives. They don't want to tell us, but they know. The underworld is brewing up poison gas and they know it."

"I don't think . . ."

"My point is that life has changed. Life the way it was is over."

"Who can say?"

"I think about my own life and I worry the best part may be behind me. I don't know, of course. Anything could happen. But let's say the best is over. I could end up poor, living in some godforsaken hole when I get older. That happens to actors all the time. You can get trapped in some terrible life and it would go on and on being terrible. The thing about movies, you know, is you can play a role in a movie and when someone says 'cut' you can walk away no matter what. You could be shot and bleeding or you could be alone and penniless. But when they yell 'cut' you can get up, brush yourself off, and go have a drink. If only real life were like that."

"That's a speech I've heard. What play is that from? Sorry, Bill, I shouldn't have said that. Maybe it was only something *like* something in a play."

"My point is, I'm just thirty-three years old and

the best years may be gone. That's not an age where you would expect to see your life in the third or fourth act. But mine could be."

"Thirty-three isn't old, Bill. There's a long time to go."

"Yes, that's my fear."

27.

Bill toasts the divorce

Bill was getting steady work as an extra playing cattle rustlers and bank robbers at Fox Films until he was told by a producer there was a rumor circulating that he had a drug addiction. Bill denied it but, in fact, it was true. He could not do without the laudanum he had been taking for back pain. So he vowed to throw off his dependency and sought out a physician who specialized in spine and nerve ailments.

The doctor prescribed light exercise, injections of formic acid ("Ants, which can lift buildings compared to their size, get all their energy from it"), and frequent meals of raw oatmeal and almonds chopped up and mixed with oil.

Prohibited from cooking in his rented room, Bill made arrangements with a restaurant near Fox to prepare the food. One evening, he entered as a party was going on to celebrate a woman's divorce. The woman and her three female friends were drinking, and hearing the waiter greet Bill as "my actor friend," one invited him over for a champagne cocktail. Bill accepted.

The three married women were bold. ("Hey, sweetheart, if you're looking at the menu, I've got a special menu you might want to order from.") However, the woman with the fresh divorce, Muriel, was quiet and would smile shyly at him from time to time. They had all been housewives in Burbank. Now Muriel had an apartment on Palms Boulevard, not far from where Bill was living.

They wanted to hear gossip about the movies and Bill told some truths and some lies. When he mentioned Charlie Chaplin's sixteen-year-old bride, Mildred Harris, the women made lewd comments.

It emerged at the end of the evening that Bill had no motor and had taken streetcars to the restaurant. The three married women insisted the divorced woman give him a ride home, almost presenting Bill as a present to her to top off her celebration.

Dizzy from the liquor, Muriel let Bill drive her Maxwell roadster.

"So why'd you divorce your husband?" he asked once they were on the highway.

"I'm not going to tell you."

"I'm interested in these things. Was it something he did or you did?"

"Something he didn't do. He didn't buy me a Cadillac. He couldn't. He doesn't make enough for even simple things, let alone a Cadillac."

"So he was a failure as a husband."

"Not really. He was good to me. But a man isn't much if he can't, you know, give a woman a life."

"Being good to you *is* a life. Lots of men aren't."

"Why don't you have a wife?"

"I had one. But I'm an actor and I had to travel. She couldn't put up with it. With your husband, though, my advice to you is that if he was good to you, you should have stayed with him."

"I don't know I loved him."

"Well, if he was good to you, I bet you eventually would of. When you're old, it would have been the most important thing."

When they reached her apartment, Bill helped her up the four floors of stairs, playfully carrying her the last flight, hoping the physical contact would persuade her to allow him liberties once they were inside. It did. When he laid her on the sofa, whether through intention or not, she pulled him on top of her. She asked for a back rub. He had no difficulty convincing her she would not get the full benefit without letting his hands under her blouse and chemise. When she pulled her arms tightly to her sides to prevent him from massaging anything but her back, it did not deter him. He only moved lower until his fingers found their way beneath the waist line of her drawers. From there, it was no trouble for him. Soon he whispered to her they would be better off in the bedroom and she agreed.

Afterward, Muriel complained in bed as Bill drank her scotch. She said how unhappy she was in Los Angeles, that she was originally from Boston, and it was unnatural for her to be this far west. When Bill said he was born in Boston, she saw the coincidence as a sign it was time for her to return east, before anything more happened to trap her in Los Angeles.

"We can both go," she said. "You can act in Boston. I've been to the Schubert. Their plays are wonderful. We can get a place in Brookline and you could take the trolley to the theatre each afternoon."

"They don't make movies in Boston. I'm a movie actor. Everything's out here now."

"But there's so many plays in Boston. I've been to the Tremont also, and there's probably six or eight more theatres. There's plenty of work for actors."

"Not movie acting, though, and that's what I do."

"Well, can't you take me to Boston anyway? You can stay a while and then come back if you don't like it. But you will. I promise. I can be much better in bed than this because I had some drinks and wasn't, you know, doing all I could. And I'm a great cook. Honestly."

"I can't. I'm about to start a picture and there's a contract. I'm in it for eight weeks."

She began to kiss Bill's chest now. "I'll wait eight weeks. Please, honey? I'll cook for you right here to save money, and with the extra money we can get a place nearer the trolley line, you know, in Boston, so you could get to the theatres. Oh, God, please?"

Bill knew this was the moment to leave. He pulled her arms from around him and got out of bed, saying he had to make the streetcar in order to get home, that he started work at six in the morning.

The detectives were brought to his room by the landlady the next evening. They were polite and consoling, apparently thinking Muriel's suicide would upset Bill. It only left him numb. As they described the circumstances, he went back through the things he had said to her, trying to think of any one thing that may have contributed. He decided he did not fault himself.

Muriel had made arrangements that morning for her own burial (representing herself to the mortician as her sister). She even bought an oak casket and a cemetery plot. Then she went home, closed off her kitchen, and uncoupled the gas line from her stove. Beside the body, which was found by the neighbor downstairs when her own stove began to flame wildly, was a note. "Please don't take me to the morgue." It gave the details of the funeral home arrangements.

When questioned about her, Bill told the detectives the truth, even about their activities in the bedroom, feeling that any lie might implicate him.

After they left, Bill decided he did not want to be alone, so he began dressing to go out, when there was a knock on his door. He thought it would be one of the detectives with another question. It was not. A bald, stocky man stood there. He showed a pistol, then put it back beneath his overcoat. He said he was Muriel's ex-husband. He demanded Bill go with him, and any time Bill started to protest, he would push the pistol forward from beneath his coat.

Muriel's Maxwell roadster was parked on the street and he told Bill to drive.

"Her friends said you were an actor. You must have some money. Where's your bank? Drive to your bank."

"I don't have any money."

On Venice Boulevard, each time they would pass a bank, the ex-husband would say, "Is this your bank? Is this where you keep it?'

He made Bill drive east for miles until they reached farms and orchards. The man, his voice breaking periodically, said he still loved his wife. He said Bill "had pushed her to do what she did."

"She only gave me a ride home," Bill said.

"That's not what the detectives told me. They said you took her inside. A neighbor said you were there more than a hour."

"It was someone else. Her friends at the restaurant, they can tell you she was just supposed to give me a ride home because I didn't have a machine. I don't have enough money for one. Honestly."

"Big Guy? Black hair? A blue jacket? That's what the neighbor said. And here you are. You've even got the blue jacket."

With that, the ex-husband pulled the pistol from beneath his coat and pointed it at Bill, who was beginning to panic.

"All I know is, she said she loved you very much, and this divorce thing, it didn't have anything to do with you, about you as a husband. It was just something about a Cadillac. I tried to tell her any husband who is a good husband other than some dispute about money, any husband like that, then she made a big mistake getting a divorce. I was on your side."

"You never went to her place?"

"She just gave me a ride home."

"Black hair? Blue jacket? Big guy?"

He told Bill to turn onto a dirt road. It was badly rutted and Bill had to slow enough that he realized he could jump out. At the right moment, he flung open the door and leaped, but his foot caught on a rut and turned over, sending a sharp pain up his leg. Nevertheless, he tried to run but almost instantly went down in the roadside weeds. A bone was sticking out of his sock, which was rapidly turning red.

By then, the ex-husband had grabbed the wheel. He backed up the car and ran it into Bill several times as he tried to crawl farther into the weeds. On each run, he smashed Bill at the highest speed he could achieve in such a short distance. When Bill no longer moved, he drove off. However, a hundred yards down the road, he turned and came back. To make it impossible to identify Bill, he shot all six rounds of the revolver into his face, aiming to find a feature each time that might still be distinguishable.

When Estelle's telephone number was found on Bill's body a week later, and she was called by the coroner to make an identification, it was a birthmark shaped like a clock face on Bill's stomach that confirmed it for her. Embarrassed to tell the coroner this, she instead said his ears and hair were enough to identify him.

28.

Bernhardt at home

In Paris with her husband to film a movie for Pathé Cinema in the late spring of 1920, Estelle read that Sarah Bernhardt, now seventy-five, was to make a return to the stage at her own theatre in the city. Despite having lost a leg to disease, she was to play the title role in *Athalie*, the Racine tragedy. Estelle asked friends who knew Sarah if they could obtain tickets for her. A day later, in the mail at her hotel, she found not only two tickets but also a calling card from Sarah asking her to visit.

That night, the streets by the theatre were filled with carriages and motor cars, with feathered hats, expensive jewelry, lavish gowns, top hats, and tuxedos. In the first act, when Sarah made her appearance on stage aboard a litter carried by attendants, frenzied cheering rose throughout the hall. Women wept. Even men wept in celebration.

Estelle, ever the professional, tended to maintain a critical distance throughout any stage play, picking apart the performances, improving the lines, and editing the gestures. However, as familiar to her as this performance was (she had once played the role), she found herself lost in the emotions of the play and of Bernhardt, and she was brought fully to tears when the murderous queen died.

The next afternoon, Estelle ventured to Bernhardt's residence in the city near the Porte d'Asniéres. Through a gate and down a long drive was an open court, then the home. Estelle handed the calling card to a servant and was led down a hallway. The walls were hung with furs and mounted antlers. She was told that others were also visiting, including members of the press.

Estelle was taken to a sunlit room on the second floor where Sarah, seated in a chair alongside her golden retriever, held court for a dozen people. In cabinets, on shelves, and residing on tables throughout the room was the detritus of more than five decades spent in the theatre. There were carved and sculpted busts of Sarah, plaques, citations, framed photographs, posters, and oils. Wearing a white robe, a rug of ermine thrown over her knees, Sarah turned when Estelle entered and with both arms gestured her over, extending her hands so that Estelle could grasp them.

"*Ma très chère amie,*" she said in her clipped French.

For the next few minutes, the two chatted as if no one else were in the room: the opening night, Estelle's career, the growing expense of films, and the diminishing opportunities for all but the youngest actresses. Then Sarah introduced her to the others, saying in French, "Estelle Harrison is one of my dearest friends, a star of films, and of course she began where all great actresses do, on the stage."

One among the visitors was Mme. Deschanel, the wife of France's president. It affected Estelle deeply that Sarah had given her all her attention with such people in the room. She realized she would never forget the kindness.

Later, a young newspaperman from the *New York Herald Tribune* introduced himself and asked Estelle what her purpose was in the city. In the Paris edition of the *Herald* several days later, Estelle saw this item in the "Comings and Goings" section:

> PARIS – Sarah Bernhardt, The Great Tragedienne, and Estelle Harrison, the American star of the silver sheet, were reunited this week at the home here of the renowned French actress. Having spent a season on tour together

earlier in their careers, these two grande dames of the acting arts exchanged views of the stage and screen.

By Mme. Harrison's own estimate, she has appeared in nearly three hundred motion pictures. Hers is a familiar face to anyone who habituates the movie palace. It is the opinion of this observer that she is becoming our American Bernhardt, yet it is by the flickering light and shadow of the motion picture that she has gained this elevated status.

End

Epilogue

Marion Fiske never returned to films. Through the 1920s, she continued to raise her family, finally having a daughter of her own in 1928, when she was thirty-four.

In 1937, her husband was found to have cancer, succumbing to the disease a year later. Through the 1940s, Marion remained in Connecticut, but in 1951, she moved to Pasadena, California, to be near her daughter. There she met and married James L. Hastings, a wealthy Santa Monica businessman. In later years, she was occasionally a guest lecturer at UCLA, speaking about the early years of silent films.

For his book, *Silence was Golden*, Roger Evans interviewed Marion, who recalled her start in films. "I had no ambition to be a film actress, because such a thing didn't exist. We invented the occupation using our sweat and our imaginations."

She died in 1962 of a stroke suffered while playing golf in Sarasota, Florida. Her ashes were interred at the Hollywood Memorial Park Mausoleum, where Rudolph Valentino's remains also reside.

Bill Trowbridge became more famous in death than in life.

After his murder, owing to his extensive disfigurement, he was cremated and his ashes were scattered in the Pacific Ocean off Long Beach. In 1921, though, the film of his incomplete boxing picture was sold at a bankruptcy auction to a studio that added extra scenes with an actor who looked like Bill, named Fred Thomas. It was then released as a secondary title. *The Pugilists* became a minor success, but when it emerged that the lead in most scenes was not Thomas, as listed in the credits, but a murdered Bill Trowbridge, the film became a sensation.

Books and articles were written about the killing and about Bill's short, mysterious life. Marion Fiske and Bill's second wife refused all interviews about him, so because of the scarcity of information about Bill, lies became facts, which were then repeated in other writings as if true. He was the illegitimate son of Argentina's president. He was an American secret agent in World War I.

He secretly made millions in the stock market, all of which he left to hospitals that served the poor.

In 1922, it was discovered that two weeks before his death, the *Los Angeles Times* had published an article about the hardships of out-of-work actors, in which Bill was interviewed but was misidentified as "Bob Trowbridge." However, the accompanying photograph proved it was him.

He was quoted as saying, "Hollywood is a place where dreams can happen. But right now, the business mentality has taken over. It's how most of the people who run these studios think. Only money matters. But that thinking is on the way out, as the people who care about pictures, about their being good, the actors like me mainly, will win out in time. They'll run everything before too long. And I know I'll be there when it happens."

Estelle Harrison moved between the stage and screen for the rest of her life, enjoying great success as a character actress in the 1930s and 1940s in talking films. She was the archetypical society matron or wise mother in dozens of films for Twentieth Century Fox and Paramount during this period.

She and her husband, Howard Drew, starred on

Broadway in 1947 in *The Quality of the Emersons*, a play that they wrote themselves. It won a Casey Award for achievement in stage drama.

Estelle explained the story to the *New York Times* this way: "We are a couple so familiar with each other that we speak each other's sentences and think each other's thoughts. Yet we see each other as complete mysteries. That is my definition of love."

Howard, who was also a successful and widely recognized character actor in movies, was nominated for an Academy Award in 1948 for the role of Dr. Paulson in *The Salvage Ship*. He died in 1951 of a heart attack. Estelle called her marriage to him "the happiest in Hollywood." She died in 1956 after a short illness and is buried at Forest Lawn Glendale.

The Blanchard Brothers Film Company is the first in a series of three novels by R. D. Snowcroft about a small group of actresses and actors in the early silent film era.

The Raspberry Girl will be published later in 2007.

Pantomime will be published in 2008.

Hampshire House Publishing Co.
8 Nonotuck Street
Florence, Mass. 01062
www.hampshirehousepub.com

Printed in the United States
R2421200001B/R24212PG54184LVSX00001B/1}